# The Agency One

**Del Uvon Bates**

Published by BookLocker.com, Inc., Trenton, Georgia, U.S.A.

The characters and events in this book are fictitious. Any
similarity to real persons, living or dead, is coincidental and not
intended by the author.

Library of Congress Cataloguing in Publication Data
Bates, Del Uvon
The Agency One by Del Uvon Bates
Library of Congress Control Number: 2024905797

BookLocker.com, Inc.
2024

Dedicated to R.J. Frisch

# Chapter 1

Our story begins in Malibu, California, where twins Elaine and Lou Richard are on track for an adventure of their lives. The siblings are returning to their beginnings in a conjoined bid to take a break from their exhilarating, yet secretive, lifestyles!

Nanny Brown, who practically raised the twins since infancy, is awaiting their arrival at the Richards' Southern California home. The compassionate and dedicated sixty-eight-year-old nursemaid has always handled the family's affairs. One of her most valuable qualities is her undying discretion. Nanny Brown has been safeguarding the secrets of the family for decades, including, if not most importantly, what the twins do for work.

You see, without knowing the truth, at first glance, Elaine and Lou seem like any other twenty-six year olds trying to figure out their young adult lives. However, underneath the cover, are two highly trained agents, each skilled in their own deceptive ways. Just two twin sisters working for The International Agency [TIA].

In an attempt to momentarily step away from their elaborate lives, the twins are planning to return home and go on a vacation together.

As always, Lou is the first to arrive. Religiously checking the time on her phone throughout the day, Lou maintains a strictly followed schedule. Her visit begins with a taste of nostalgia. Nanny greets Lou at the steps of the estate, as she has always done. A warm embrace by her childhood caretaker reminds Lou of the comforts of being home. "Surprise, surprise!" Lou says as she pulls away from Nanny. "Elaine is going to be arriving late."

"The Agency?" Nanny sarcastically asks, already knowing the answer.

"Elaine is finishing up an investigation before she can officially take some time off," Lou says as she takes Nanny by the hand, strolling into what appears to be a castle of a home.

Nanny guides Lou into the kitchen, insisting she eat something. "You're too skinny, Lou. You need more meat on your bones," Nanny says as she reaches into the oven, grabbing a warm batch of freshly baked muffins.

Lou scarfs one down, thinking, *There's nothing like home cooking*, as the last bite slides down her throat and into her stomach. "I'm going to go freshen up in my room," Lou tells Nanny, who is already walking toward the hallway where Lou's bags are perched up against the wall.

"Please, Nanny," Lou says as she lunges toward her bags, almost knocking Nanny Brown out of the way. "I'm quite capable and grown now. I can carry my things myself!"

Nanny smirks, replying, "You know why they call it luggage, right? Because you've got to lug it everywhere you go!" Laughing at her own joke, she asks Lou, "Are you sure you don't want me to grab 'em?"

Lou chuckles, responding, "No, Nanny, I've got it. You don't have much help around here these days, do you?"

"Not since you and your sister were recruited by the TIA. They won't allow me any extra help other than the maid, chef, and groundskeeper," Nanny replied. Nanny, also bound to secrecy by the agency, can only work the property with limited secret cleared support personnel.

"We'll have to change that. You shouldn't be stuck doing all this work on your own," Lou says, knowing how hard her childhood caretaker works to keep the house in order.

"Oh, no! The TIA has these rules for a reason Lou. Plus, your parents travel so often, there's really not too much work to get done around here these days," Nanny replies.

Lou smiles down at Nanny as she makes her way up the spiral staircase, bags in each hand. "Well, regardless of the agency's policies, please keep what I said in mind. We can get you more help here if needed."

After ascending the stairs, Lou walks into her room, tossing her suitcases onto the bench at the end of her large bed. Lou freshens up in her ensuite and then moves to sit on a chair beside an open window. She slowly runs her hands up her legs, smoothing the Coco Chanel body cream into her skin. Lou slips into something more comfortable, and makes her way downstairs, just in time to catch the sunset. Golden in its glory, Lou stares into the godly horizon remembering why she missed home.

As the sun sinks into the ocean, Lou thinks of Elaine, who is preoccupied by the duties of the Agency. She gives Elaine a call to check in.
"Hello?" Elaine says frantically as she answers her sister's phone call.

"Well, hello Elaine, glad I called at a good time," Lou jokingly responds back to Elaine. "Sorry, I didn't mean to bother you when you're busy. I just wanted to check in and see when you will be arriving home?"

Elaine lets out a stressful, yet sincere laugh. "Oh, Lou. It's so good to hear from you. I'm going to be later than I anticipated.

The last mission went long. I'm just now getting back to Arizona so I can tie up some things with my latest property acquisition and feed Benny before I head to the airport."

"See, now what did I tell you about getting a cat? How do you expect to work for the TIA and maintain your busy cover as a real estate agent, all the while having a pet to look after? You're already too busy as it is," Lou says to Elaine who is rolling her eyes on the other end of the phone.

"Lou, with the crazy lives we live through the TIA, Benny is one of the few things that keep me grounded amid the chaos. He makes me feel like I'm a normal human, living a normal life," Elaine replies to Lou. "But I do wish I had Nanny here with me so I could get some of this stuff done faster."

Shortly, before being called away on her last mission, Elaine had invested in a new property. After purchasing some new furniture and knickknacks so the house could be staged, she hired a cleaning company to thoroughly sanitize it so it could be put on the market for resale. With the mission over, Elaine finds herself back in Arizona with several things commanding her attention.

"Alright, Lou. I'll give you or Nanny a call when I'm on my way to the airport. I've got to scramble to get things done here so Benny and I can make my flight. I love you, Bye for now," Elaine said.

Del Uvon Bates

"I love you too," Lou says as she hangs up the phone. After nibbling on the World-Class crackers and cheese left out by Nanny, Lou makes her way inside. She finds Nanny alongside a wooden box labeled "imported" in the kitchen.

"What's this?" Lou asks as her curiosity peaks.

"Wine," Nanny replies. "A whole case of it. Mark Andrews heard you were coming home and brought over this case of mixed bottles earlier, including your favorite Sauvignon Blanc."

Mark Andrews, one of Lou's romantic interests, has been in love with her since the day they met in the 5th grade. "He was very disappointed earlier when you had not yet arrived...as was I," Nanny tells Lou. "Mark said he would stop by a little later when they got home."

Nanny pulls three bottles of wine from the case, asking Lou, "Would you like me to decant the 2013 Red Opus or uncork the 2019 Chardonnay or the Sauvignon Blanc? But, knowing you . . . I better whip up a martini."

"You know me too well," Lou replies, as she grabs a couple of glasses from the cabinet and sits back down to reminisce with Nanny. "You know, I remember when I was a young girl...I would sneak a sip of your martini when you weren't looking. I always admired the way you seemed to know it all. You made everything seem so sophisticated. I really wanted to be a woman you would approve of when I grew up. You taught me that brains, combined with class is the perfect recipe for a well-adjusted, independent person. I adore you for that!"

Nanny gives Lou a warm embrace. "You know how proud I am of you, right?" Nanny asks as she wipes away several tears that have made their way from her eyes. "Never stop being you, Lou. No one else does it better."

With Elaine in Arizona, Nanny mentioned to Lou, "Whatever you do, when Elaine arrives, you must promise me that you will take a vacation together. Both of you have been working too long at TIA without a vacation. I can tell you from experience, TIA will take advantage of you if you allow them to. That is why I semi-retired, well at least from the University to become a Nanny for your parents. Others would say, working twenty-four seven is not their idea of retirement. To me, you twins are my children and I am what one might call a stand-in for your parents, plus I get paid for it."

Lou looked at Nanny and asked, "Would you like to split the last bit of martini with me and then turn in for the night? I'll leave a note for the maid to clean things up when she arrives in the morning." They enjoyed the rest of their drink and joining hands went up to bed.

## Chapter 2

Nanny was up early before the maid arrived, so she cleaned up last night's mess.

The maid entered the kitchen and Nanny instructed her to set up the casual food bar in the outdoor patio that faced the ocean. "Be sure and set out the silver dishes for cold food, as well as for hot serve. Probably service for four people just in case someone stops by. In the flower cooler you'll find there are several flower arrangements for the area. We should also open the bar for breakfast drinks."

About 8:30 a.m., Lou entered the kitchen giving Nanny a kiss on the cheek. She was immediately handed a cup of piping hot black coffee. Lou sat on the stool and proceeded to talk to Nanny as she whisked Lou's favorite pancake batter.

The cook arrived in time to take over the kitchen duties and sent Lou and Nanny out of his kitchen. "There is fresh coffee and whatever you want to pass the time, while I create food fit for queens," the cook said.

They all laughed as they made their way to the patio. They sat down and took a sip of their drinks and both said with a sigh, "Wish Elaine was here."

Nanny's cell phone rang and it was Elaine calling from Arizona. "Your ears must be burning? Lou and I just said we wished you were here."

Elaine replied with a smile in her voice, "I'll be flying out shortly to visit you. I called to tell you I'll fly into Santa Monica airport and TIA will have a car waiting. They have my itinerary should you need it and will inform you of my ETA."

Before she hung up, she remembered an earlier conversation she had with TIA, asking her to take a case. Elaine's cell phone rang the special ring only TIA had. The voice on the other end asked, "Are you able to answer our questions at this time?" Elaine softly answered, "Yes, but briefly." The voice continued, "We need you to handle a specific case (which meant...top secret with special circumstances)." Elaine said, "That can be arranged if I can do it while on vacation." They agreed.

"Lou, I can't wait to hear what you have decided about going on a trip with me. You'll have to travel my way instead of first class like you usually do. Little ole me cannot, for obvious reasons travel that way, as I have to be less conspicuous," Elaine laughed.

Elaine added, "Nanny, I have a message for you from Harry. He has a package of goodies from TIA (objects for self-security beyond physical contact). He'll be traveling with me."

Harry was a university professor where Nanny taught before semi-retirement. They both did work at the university for the TIA, collecting valuable information. Harry was always a part of the twin's life, as long as they could remember.

"Nanny, Harry would like to take you out for dinner this evening. Oh, the movers are here. Sorry, I have to go," Elaine abruptly hung up.

Elaine was having boxes delivered to the turn-key home she had purchased in Arizona. She had them place the boxes in the specific rooms where she needed them to begin staging the home for sale.

Lou called Elaine back when she thought the movers would be finished and said, "With Nanny and Harry gone we have the house to ourselves and, my dear Elaine, it's time for fun and games for a day or two. After a couple of days at the estate, we can then start on our trip."

Lou continued: "I checked the road map and I would like to travel along the California coast and up to Washington state where a friend of mine has a small cottage in Copalis Beach, WA. We can stay there awhile and see the Fourth of July festivities. I understand everyone who's anyone goes to the beach. There are lots of local food trucks, bands, and hopefully we can make a new friend or two. On a different note, is Harry seeing that we have a car full of goodies?"

Elaine answered, "Of course he is."

Lou continued with excitement, "We are traveling a long way and I hope to stop now and then to shop. You know I'm not the camper type, so a nice quiet hotel and good restaurants with great food will help make up for my traveling in a car."

They both chuckled.

Lou mentioned to Elaine, "Your specialty as a forensic psychologist and criminal psychologist, must be the reason you are needed for that TIA case."

Elaine replied, "Now Lou, you know we can't discuss cases with each other! It should be a no brainer though."

Lou didn't tell Elaine that she was also on a case. Lou and Elaine, as twins, always seemed to sense when each other were involved in top secret activities (cases).

Lou was happy her specialties required undercover traveling in jets...first class all the way, of course. "The office thinks of me as an expert in foreign affairs or wealthy eye candy who takes notes and translates in many languages for the person she is assigned to. I am expected to protect and keep my clients away from the media without alerting anyone that there is 'more afoot than meets the eye.' (to quote Sherlock). My work is top secret even to the person that is escorting me to fancy functions."Lou said, "We'll talk more about the trip when you get here."

Lou's assignment is to ascertain the whereabouts of Diane Lane.

Diane Lane also works for the TIA as a field agent. Diane had a hunch about an illegal activity (her gut feelings usually proved worthwhile). Diana did not want to disclose her hunch to her bosses, so she requested a vacation. Why she got this feeling she couldn't explain to TIA just yet.

The day before she was due back in the office, she left an encrypted message stating she would be extending her leave for reasons she'd explain later. This request was received two weeks earlier. "Later" had not come as soon as TIA wanted. She wasn't answering her phone and there was no signal coming from her tracer. Worried that Diane may be in trouble, they contacted Lou. Lou has been assigned to look into this critical situation concerning one of their important agents.

Diane lives in an apartment with a girl she met at a local hangout, The Purple Pub and Grill, in the area of Ocean Shores,

Washington. She will have to start her search there, hopefully, speaking with Diane's roommate.

TIA wished Diane had left some clue as to what she was being so secretive about. Lou has a chance of finding out while posing as a tourist with a friend while on holiday.

Elaine and Harry are on their way to California with Elaine piloting the jet. They land at the Santa Monica airport and make way to the terminal for private airplanes. Harry says to Elaine, "Wait till you see your transportation."

There, in their special parking space, was a Range Rover Sport Dynamic SE from England. Harry said, "I will explain some of its added features when we are on our way to your estate." They loaded the Rover and got the okay from security to leave for Malibu.

Elaine was all excited with the color of the "Dead Black" exterior paint on the Rover. This paint absorbs all light with no reflection. Elaine entered the vehicle and was truly surprised with the luxurious interior highlights. Twelve-way driver's seat and ten-way front passenger seat, heated front seats, ebony-grained leather seats, auto high beam assist, led headlights with signature DLR, adaptive cruise control, and keyless entry.

It was four-wheel-drive, sported bulletproof windows, a reinforced/bulletproof chassis, and a GPS tracker, which tracks anything that nears the car. It will send a signal detailing what it is with the information going directly to TIA.

TIA immediately notifies the operator of the Range Rover of pending or pressing problems. Elaine can hear what the problem areas are, what it is, and which switch to push to eliminate this situation. There is radar, lasers, and jammers to interrupt other electrical systems with cell phone reception in and out; flat proof tires from bullets to running over objects that might disrupt the operation of the rover. If necessary, the car will automatically switch to high-speed travel with automatic driving assistance if needed. "To tell you all the things I have installed, all at once, is too much," Harry said.

Elaine drove through Santa Monica and down to the Pacific Coast Highway to the estate. The car was a dream to drive, Elaine told Harry.

Harry jumped out of the car as Nanny was running towards him and they embraced. Lou and Elaine hugged each other and all four went into the house. "Drinks all around?" queried Nanny.

"Do I have to tell you," they all said in harmony, "you bet!" They ordered their drinks and Harry stepped in to help.

# Chapter 3

Harry and Nanny decided to go to dinner and make it a long weekend. They would stay in a local bed and breakfast for a couple of nights. That decided, Elaine and Lou winked at each other and said they were going to stay at the estate until after the weekend and check out the local haunts. Nanny laughed and said softly, "Now girls, you may think I don't know what you mean by checking out the local haunts. Go ahead and go upstairs and make your plans for the evening. Lou, I know you are dying to call Mark, so go ahead."

Elaine went to her room which was adorned with a large bookshelf filled with books, a fragrant flower arrangement, a full drink bar, and snacks. By the doors going onto the veranda was a set of athletic equipment. Elaine always exercised to keep fit so she could handle any confrontation she may experience while on her cases. She mostly worked solo, so being in top shape was a must.

Both she and her sister were linguists and well-traveled. They were top notch historians and knew the history of nearly every country.

Harry had shown the goodies he brought for the girls to Nanny. She knew for sure there was more to this trip than just a vacation.

With both of the twins working, this would mean they would have to be aware of their surroundings at all times.

"Harry, you must insist they never are without the new goodies you brought them. You must explain to them thoroughly as to the use of their bracelet and to never take it off. It could save their lives. Make sure you put it on them yourself so they can never remove it, nor can anyone else. With them traveling so far, I want you to put mine on and make it so I can tell if something is wrong. Those jewels look so authentic. You would never guess that one changes color when it detects hidden spy devices. It can detect all hidden wired or wireless magnetic field or radio wave gadgets. The other one has a transmitter that automatically changes color when there is another agent in their vicinity. This alerts them/you not to acknowledge you know them; or if you do not, it may mean they are a danger to you in some way. The other jewel tells you to go somewhere private so you can make a conference call to TIA immediately," Nanny said extremely impressed.

Harry included more information with pride, "The black stone is simply the most important of all. Field agents are all given this stone. If you are in danger, you press the black stone while turning it to the left counter-clockwise and it will turn 'white.' This will notify any agent in range you need immediate assistance. They will, once receiving this signal, turn their emergency tracer stone clockwise, which will inform them of your position. They are to drop everything to reach you and see that you are safely extracted. This stone is one of the most important...in that everyone is responsible for each other. One of the first things we learn if we are accepted by TIA is we are a team. Agents lives come first and foremost."

Other goodies consist of cameras that are incorporated in rings, pens, ankle bracelets, buttons, and earrings—just to name a few. The tube of lip gloss has the ingredient benzodiazepine, which when a small amount comes into contact with a person's skin, they will shortly pass out for twenty minutes. When they awake, they will not remember anything," Harry said.

The girls talked to Mark and he informed them he had a friend visiting from London. Would they mind if he joined them for dinner, dancing, and other activities?

"Casual, elegant dress for this evening," Lou said to Elaine. Elaine knew she meant no tennis shoes.

"Don't worry Lou, I won't embarrass you when I meet Mark's friend, I promise. This isn't my first blind date. Maybe, it will be the first one I enjoy!" said Elaine.

They went downstairs together to see what goodies Harry had obtained for them. He showed them the goodies, along with an explanation of how each item was to be used. Harry put the bracelets on the twins, including one for Nanny and himself. "Now ladies, are you sure you know how to use the stones? I want you to commit the instructions to memory." The twins smiled at each other as both were blessed with great memories. Some might even say they had photographic minds.

Lou said, "Nanny, as far as anyone knows, we are on vacation and that includes Mark and anyone that might inquire. But then, you and Harry probably wrote the book of agents 'do's and 'don'ts' for TIA."

Lou and Elaine hugged and kissed both of the lovebirds and saw them on their way, wishing them a great weekend.

Lou said, "Sister dear, shall we go up and make ourselves irresistible for the boys so they don't know what hit them?"

Shortly, the bell rang and Lou answered the intercom, "Come in and make yourselves at home. Mark, you know your way around, we will be down soon." Lou and Elaine waited fifteen minutes and then made their grand entrance down the spiral staircase. Both guys were staring at them with their mouths wide open. Mark quickly made the introduction of his English business associate/friend to Elaine. "Elaine, I would like you to meet Albert Downing."

Albert stuck out his hand and said to Elaine, "Please call me Al, for short."

Elaine said, "Well Al, since you are a Downing, are you from number 10 Downing Street?"

Al laughed and handed Elaine and Lou a glass of champagne, walking them outside to watch the sun go down into the ocean. Mark suggested they go downtown and take in the sights and sounds. "I didn't make reservations Lou. We can always get in without a reservation, if you know what I mean."

With a smile on her face, she looked at Mark with a knowing wink and said, "Money talks."

They got into Mark's limousine and he ordered Franko, his driver, to head to Santa Monica's main part of town. Mark asked Lou and Elaine if they liked seafood. Lou said, "Nothing better than fresh seafood."

Mark pressed the intercom and requested Franko drive them to the Blue Plate Oysterette on Ocean Avenue. Mark touched Al on the arm and said to him, "I am sure you will enjoy this place as well."

Lou said softly to Elaine, "This is a place where if you had to ask the price you couldn't afford it. Mark is really trying to show off."

Elaine said with a grin, "I certainly hope Al likes seafood. Coming from London it is definitely not his usual fish and chips."

They were seated at a corner table overlooking the bay. Peter, their waiter, was very efficient and said he would send over the sommelier.

Mark ordered wine and Al suggested some appetizers to start. They asked Peter to surprise them with a selection of appetizers as they looked over the main courses. The white Chablis wine was served, Mark sampled it, and nodded it was satisfactory. Peter served four different types of appetizers. Scampi in a lemon and garlic butter sauce, marinated raw tuna on sesame toasts, lightly breaded fried calamari, and lobster stuffed mushrooms. Enough for all to enjoy.

They took their time getting to know each other through conversation and when Peter thought it was time, the table was cleared, their main course delivered, with more wine placed in the ice bucket.

The evening flew by and once they left the restaurant, they decided to return to Mark's digs and have after dinner drinks along with a walk on the beach. Lou and Elaine took off their shoes while Mark and Al did the same, except they rolled their pant legs up to enjoy the ocean.

The couples laughed as they waded in the ocean and finally headed back to Mark's place. Lou and Elaine picked up their shoes and purses they had left on the path leading to Mark's abode. Hand in hand, the couples headed for the house. On the way, Elaine's phone rang the special TIA sound and in her formal voice she answered. Knowing she was not alone, they requested she get to a place where they could talk freely.

In many ways, the call came at the right time. She did not want her evening to continue with Al. Not because she didn't enjoy his company, but because, unlike Lou, she didn't know him that well. Lou looked at Elaine and she held the phone at her side meaning she had to get back and return her call in private. Taking the signal, Lou told Mark to call Franko to take Elaine home as she had an emergency to take care of. Mark explained to Al the change in plans. Al asked Elaine, "Would you like me to accompany you home." Elaine said, "No, as unfortunately, it's a business call which needs to be dealt with promptly and these calls could take up a lot of time."

They walked Elaine to the car. Al gave her a hug and a light kiss on her neck which she enjoyed more than she thought she would. Al bent and whispered in her ear, "Sorry you have to leave, but I do understand, till tomorrow." He waved as Franko drove off.

Lou said to Mark and Al, "I'll call home and leave a voicemail for the cook to come up with something special for us for brunch tomorrow. Bring your swimsuits if you want to go swimming and then we can visit downtown Malibu, as it has been a long time since I was there."

Mark laughed and said, "It's much the same with the exception of more shops, cars and lots of people."

Al went back into the house and Mark told him, "Make yourself comfortable. When you're ready to turn in, your suite is up the stairs to the end of the hall on the left. Upon wakening, the morning staff will have breakfast ready, placed outside your door. If you need anything else, just request it. The newspapers from both our area and England will be placed on your tray. We'll be up early, as Lou has business to take care of and wants to be taken back to her home to check things out."

Lou and Mark held hands as they went upstairs and light music came from their suite. There on the oversized bed was a box with a rose on it and a tag that read "Lou." Mark made his way to the shower. Since Lou could not wait, she sat on the bed and excitedly opened the box. She looked up and saw Mark was rubbing his hair dry with a towel. He also had a towel around his waist watching her, and he said, "Lou, you look like a little girl with her very first gift. It is always such fun giving you something just to see the expression on your face. I hope you like it, as it was made special for you in Paris, France, by an up-and-coming designer and owner of the latest boudoir boutique. Well, my lovely lady, with green eyes! You must let me see how you look in it!"

She hugged Mark and he held her tightly for a moment and she whispered in his ear in her soft sensuous voice, "Hold that thought. A quick shower...I'll be right back."

What seemed like a lifetime, Mark waited. He was sitting up in bed covered only with pearly white satin sheets. If anyone knew how to rouse someone's attention it was Lou. She came into the room slowly with a light ocean breeze tousling her hair and the moon shining bright into the room. The fine sheer silk robe moving as she walked, accented the greenish hue of the negligee. Mark said, "Lou come here so we can get back to my earlier thoughts of you in that negligee." With her come-hither smile and gracefulness, they embraced and the night turned into morning way too soon.

Mark got up first and there was a cart waiting in the hall with an icy cool pitcher of mimosas, dark roast coffee, today's newspaper, and a note from Al saying, "Come down and join me outside, enjoying the California sunshine. Nothing like England this time of year."

After a short repeat of last night, Lou and Mark showered and joined Al. "Sorry Elaine had business to handle last evening," Al said, sheepishly. "But then I will get to see her today."

Lou noticed a look of puppy love all over his face.

"How long are you staying before you leave on your vacation?" Mark asked.

Lou said, "I hope a few more days. We'll see, as Elaine is in charge of this vacation."

Mark laughed and said, "I just can't picture you traveling in a car when I would be happy to fly you both in my jet. You could spend more time together."

Lou laughed and said: "It was not her idea of fun with the exception that we both enjoy seeing how the other half lives. Of course, traveling in the latest Range Rover with all the bells and whistles isn't like being in just any car. Elaine loves the outdoors and would have me sleeping in a tent if she could. She compromised and said we'll stop often to see the small towns and stay at good hotels where there are nice restaurants available. We can check out museums, antique stores, and enjoy the locals. Harry picked up the Range Rover when he was in England and had it shipped over here and delivered it to Santa Monica airport for Elaine to bring to our place here after flying in. Nanny had Harry select our transportation so she would know we would be safe. It'll be just like Elaine to go off road to try out the four-wheel-drive feature."

Al said, "Did I hear you correctly, that Elaine flew the plane to Santa Monica airport? Wow! She is quite a gal."

"Oh! You don't know the half of it. She can do just about anything, and does," Lou said and winked at Mark with a twinkle in her eye and smile on her face.

Lou suggested they get their things together for a swim and brunch at her place and then later have some fun in town.

## Chapter 4

They enjoyed their brunch and the pool for a few hours and then decided to go to the pool house for a refreshing shower. There were several separate suites to accommodate everyone. The maid had everything set out for their enjoyment.

There were flowers everywhere because the ladies have always enjoyed the smell of fresh flowers. As girls, Nanny always made them flower rings to put on their beautiful hair. Funny, Lou has sunny blond hair and Elaine has reddish blond hair so the flowers had to be different. Elaine liked gardenias and Lou loved her cymbidium orchids.

Mark said, "Well, shall we proceed to town and gather in the old and new sights. I called Franko earlier and he may be waiting out front for us." They walked hand in hand to the waiting limo. Franko held the doors open and made sure they were comfortable. He had soft music with a swing beat playing. Finding a place to park left Mark with no choice but to have Franko let them off downtown so they could walk around. Mark would let him know where to pick them up later.

Meanwhile, Harry and Nanny were enjoying their late brunch and reminiscing about the twins as little girls. Nanny recalled growing the orchids herself, in pots in an area along the side of the house. Lou always commented on how beautiful the cymbidiums looked and of course she thought she was the special twin with her very own orchids.

Harry spoke about how he had the landscapers plant gardenias. They grew large and beautiful, which just so happened to be Elaine's favorite flower, and she too thought they were just for her. Funny how that happens sometimes.

Harry enjoyed playing golf, studying judo, taekwondo, and other self-defense arts with Elaine. She was always so competitive in what she did and she was good at it. Harry knew it would give her the knowledge she needed if she planned to follow in her parents' footsteps.

Nanny said, "Lou was so good with the arts, but even better at being a lady. Not necessarily the athletic type. That is why I drilled into her brain as much education as she could absorb, like languages and history. This was certainly her forte. Both girls went to separate universities, got their master's degrees and were top of their class. It's funny, their master's were in different subjects, but certainly helped them when TIA invited them to follow in their parents' footsteps. Each in their separate fields."

Nanny and Harry held hands and Harry said proudly, "When you left your job at the university for this one to be a nanny, it made me wonder if you had done the right thing. Never in my wildest dreams did I realize what enjoyment it would bring to both of us. To quote a friend, 'Ahh! Life is good.'" They both had their last sip of coffee and smiling said it was time to return to the estate.

Lou and Elaine were enjoying ice cream sodas when their phones rang almost at the same time. The girls excused themselves and went in different secluded areas to talk to TIA. They came back and in unison they said, "We have to get back home, duty calls."

Mark called Franko and informed him where to pick them up.

It was quiet on the way home from town as the twins were preoccupied by what TIA needed to discuss. "I guess they don't know what to say. Just like a woman!" Al said to Mark softly, "Nothing to say when you want them to talk."

Mark replied, "I guess you have never been around businesswomen, let alone twins. They have a position in life even I do not ask what it is. I just know, when their boss calls, they drop everything and head for the storm."

Finally, the silence was broken and Elaine said to Mark and Al, "We will have to call it a day. We only hope Nanny and Harry are not so far away that we can't say goodbye because when we leave it may be quite a while until our vacation is over."

Al looked at Mark and again spoke softly, "Some vacation, huh?"

Franko pulled up the long driveway with the fresh smell of the ocean breeze. As faith would have it, Nanny and Harry must have come home early because their car was parked out front.

Lou said, "Well, will you look at that. Nanny and Harry came home sooner than expected."

Mark said with a frown on his face, "Darn."

Lou knew what he was thinking and she leaned close to his ear and softly blew in as she spoke, "Me too!"

Franko stopped the car and ran around to open the doors to let them out. Coming down the front steps was Harry. "We just got home ourselves...are you home for the evening or is this a pit stop?"

Elaine spoke first and sadly said, "Business calls and we have to leave on vacation sooner than we thought. We are hoping to be able to see Al and Mark upon our return if Al is still in town."

They all got out of the car and walked up the front into the house. The maid took the things the girls bought and took them up to their rooms.

Nanny said to Harry, "Why the long faces? Did something go wrong?"

Harry said, "You know what happened, TIA."

"Well, we can't have anyone leave without relaxing on the veranda. All of us have to talk and make the most of the situation, as always!" Nanny asked the cook and maid to fix some drinks and appetizers that would cheer them up.

Harry mixed the drinks, the maid fixed the table, and the cook fixed a plate of sandwiches, finger food, condiments, and a mixture of desserts. Harry kept the drinks coming.

Harry asked the maid to take a tray of food to Franko or to invite him into the kitchen as they might be awhile. "No booze my dear, with a wink, he's driving."

They were soon laughing, joking, and talking about when Lou, Elaine and Mark were young and the things they got into. Al was laughing so hard and said, "I should have been so lucky. In England children were seen and not heard. Of course, what they didn't know didn't hurt us." He said, "British kids have different things to do than the American youth. When you get down to it, all of us had a great childhood, I think."

Mark, having gone through this before with the girls' short holidays, knew it was time to call it a day and let them pack and do whatever they had to do to get ready for the "vacation."

Al took his lead and reached for Elaine's hand and Mark took Lou's. They said their good-byes, thanked Nanny and Harry for their hospitality, and strolled out the front door. Harry went on the intercom and told the kitchen help to tell Franko to go to the front to take Mark and Al back to his place.

While waiting for Franko to bring the limo up front, Mark and Al both embraced their dates and said their goodbyes. Mark hugged Lou and kissed her several times while speaking softly, he wished she didn't need to leave. Telling her to take care of herself and call him if she needed him. They lingered in each other's embrace.

Al held Elaine a long time before he kissed her as though they knew each other forever. He wished her a safe trip and God speed. Al asked, "May I call you some time, or don't you take calls when on business?"

Elaine replied, "I think I will have to let Mark know when you can contact me. Sometimes, in my line of work I don't know where I will be and answering the phone is not an easy thing to do. I do want to get together, possibly at a function in England. Who knows?" Elaine left it at that...sometimes keeping them guessing is better all the way around. The ladies waved as the men went back down the long road to pacific coast highway to Mark's home.

Lou and Elaine were in a hurry to talk to Nanny and explain their schedule as best they could. Checking their goodies and especially their transmitters they looked a little concerned. Well, at least Lou did, as she was not used to traveling on the road. Harry said to Nanny and the girls, "Don't worry, I have given you all the goodies needed. With your training and the Range Rover, whatever you are involved in will be a piece of cake. Remember, safety first, stay alert while traveling, and let the car handle any problems that arise with the help of TIA."

Elaine and Lou had their belongings packed and ready to be loaded in the Rover. Elaine said to Lou, "I don't know about your case, but mine allows me to enjoy myself with a few stops along the way."

"Mine also," Lou said.

Harry loaded the Range Rover and made sure he packed the things he thought they might need closer to the front of the door for easy access.

Nanny had a care package full of anything they might want. Hot coffee, lots of water and snacks.

Elaine and Lou got in the car. They double checked to make sure they had everything they needed: cellphones, phone chargers, laptops, and travel guides. "Looks like we are off," Elaine said. They waved good-bye to Nanny and Harry.

They headed towards Highway 101 and then travelled onto the Pacific Coast Highway, the most scenic route. As Elaine drove, Lou was enjoying figuring out all of the bells and whistles in their new ride.

# Chapter 5

"Well here goes nothing." Lou said. The girls laughed and were glad to be on their way. There would be fun and games after they finished their respective cases.

By three o'clock in the morning, the traffic was getting very heavy. Lou started getting drowsy, so she adjusted her seat for comfort and took a short nap. Lou had great confidence in Elaine's driving skills. Elaine smiled and was reassured this was going to be a good trip. She thought to herself, *When Lou wakes up, we can stop for a cup of gourmet coffee.*

The weather was such that it will prove to be easy driving. The Rover certainly lives up to its hype. It's easy handling, goes over rough spots with little bouncing, if any, and overall comfort.

Elaine was enjoying looking at all the goodies installed on the dash. A flashing dot appeared with a very brief message. "Contact TIA and use your earphone. Confidential, for your ears only!" Then the dot started flashing faster. "I guess they thought I needed to reply ASAP. My handler Bill must want me to know it's super important."

Elaine put in her earphones and immediately was connected to TIA. Bill's voice said, "Come in, come in!"

Elaine laughed and said, "I am only in a Range Rover, not a truck, ole buddy."

Bill said, "Well, I know it's you answering. Only you would laugh at my jokes, however, this is no joke. This case is special and confidential. You are to go to the local agency. The town and address will be indicated on your dash. Once there, you are to show your credentials where you'll be presented with a package. Once you return to the Rover, Lou should go in and check to see if there is a package waiting for her. In your package, you will be apprised of a person of interest involved in serial killings. The news media and public are not aware of these murders. To avoid public panic, it is to remain secret until further notice. You must take every precaution to stay unnoticed, while appearing to be tourists. Being on separate cases, you will probably have completely different instructions. Elaine, regardless, you are in control of the traveling and must follow...to the letter...what further agencies to stop at, as well as your lodgings and eating establishments. You and Lou seem to read each other's minds which is a great advantage because this pervert is dangerous.

Lou will suggest she wants to shop along the way at certain towns and stores. Do so without question. Go your own way on these stops and do not interfere with her shopping. During these stops, use whatever excuse necessary not to be considered friends or acquaintances with each other. This is for your own safety! You will see that there is a B&B, along with their address which you will stay in when you stop in Grants Pass, Oregon."

# Chapter 6

Elaine and Lou went through a gourmet coffee drive-thru and got two iced mocha coffees and headed to the bed and breakfast.

This is a hangout for hunters and fishermen all year round. The twins separately went into the office fifteen minutes apart to register and get their room keys. The front desk enquired if they needed bellhop services to handle their luggage. Both Elaine and Lou declined. They were placed two cabins apart.

As it was early afternoon and they were to stay two nights, Elaine called the office and asked about the all-inclusive dining package. "We have arranged that you will join the other guests that are also lodging at the bed and breakfast. Dining is at 5:00 p.m." The man said.

Elaine put on her jogging clothes and went for a run around the lodge and down by the water. As she was enjoying a pause for a drink of water, a brown and white dog came over to her, sat down, and started looking at her, wanting her to notice him. He gave a little bark. There was a distinguished tall man with striking blue eyes and a lovely smile who walked up and said softly, "I hope Mavie is not bothering you. You are safe! He just likes to be noticed and if he is lucky, he might get a treat. My name is Jay." He handed Mavie a treat. "Are you staying here at the lodge or just out for a run?"

Elaine introduced herself and said, "I'm staying in one of the cabins for a few nights. Then on the road again. It's vacation time for me." She thanked him for the nice conversation, excused herself and said she wanted to get a little more exercise in before dinner.

Jay and Mavie watched her jog off and they went back to the dock and sat down to enjoy the fishing. "They're not biting," he said to his dog as Mavie looked into the water like he wanted to go in. "No Mavie, not while I'm fishing," he laughed and his dog just sat and looked at him as if he could change Jay's mind.

Elaine contacted Lou and told her she would see her later. Lou said the front desk had called her and told her dinner was at five. "I can see this is time for roughing it and not dressing up."

Elaine laughed at Lou and said, "Casual attire or for you, working clothes. I will wear pants and a shirt with tennis shoes. Remember, I understand we'll be at separate tables, so we may not even be able to talk at dinner. We can contact each other after dinner and see if we gleaned any of the latest local news."

Lou said she needed to go shopping and would check out the other shops in the area tomorrow.

Elaine showered and made herself a drink out of the cooler Nanny and Harry so graciously stocked for their trip. Lou is also equipped with snacks and drinks to her liking in her cooler. Elaine enjoyed her drink while sitting on the porch watching the boats on the water and the old guys going into the local pub to play darts, drink beer, and tell their much-elaborated fish stories of their latest catch.

Looking at her cell phone and checking out her goodies, to be sure, Lou was okay. She brushed her hair and her teeth and headed for the dining room.

*What a lovely evening it's going to be,* she thought. A slight breeze came up from the water, blowing the fall leaves back and forth on large branches—some of them falling to the ground for the grounds keeper to rake up in the morning. She thought this would truly be a pleasant place to spend a few days vacation. Too bad the case comes first. *Perhaps when it is over, we can stop back here and enjoy some time like we did when we were younger.*

Elaine reached the dining-room before Lou. As she entered, the waitress said her table was ready. As she made her way to her seat, Jay saw her and suggested she join them at his table. She looked at the waitress and she said go ahead as there's room. We have selected several tables that you would enjoy and this happens to be one of them. As Jay held her chair out for her, she saw Lou enter. Lou turned everyone's head with her leather boots, Levi's, and Robin's egg blue Valentino casual shirt (or should we say, blouse). Lou looked around and saw Elaine at a table near one of the three tables suggested. Lou chose one closest to her sister. One of the men quickly got up and held a chair out for her to seat herself on. She smiled and thanked him and introduced herself. He in turn introduced all the others at the table.

The dinner was a home style dinner with a waitress for each large table. The first course was a fresh garden salad with home grown lettuce, tomatoes, radishes, cucumbers, and spring onions. Several dressings were placed on a tray that swiveled and they chose the one they wanted. The special of the night was fresh grilled trout with fresh mixed vegetables, twice baked potatoes, and homemade biscuits. The food was better than Lou had expected for a B&B. Elaine heard Lou laughing at the fishermen jokes and having a truly enjoyable time.

Elaine was talking to everyone at the table; however, the conversation between her and Jay was more interesting and they began to converse quietly between themselves. The dinner seemed to go by fast and the busboy removed the dishes. It was announced the chef's special cinnamon apple pie with vanilla ice cream, cheese, and whipped cream was their dessert. Coffee or tea was also served. They were invited to go to the pub and enjoy after dinner drinks if so desired.

It was not surprising to see the true fisherman opting to go to their respective cabins so they could get up before daybreak and find their favorite fishing spot. It was fun hearing some say to each other, "Who is ready for one more beer before bed?" Most of them headed for the bar because they wanted to find out what each one thought was their best bait or what rod and reel they might use.

One fisherman stated he always went to Marty's Place before starting his day fishing. "Marty's Place has everything you would expect to need in a store. Just like the old west movies. Mercantile extraordinary! It is a mini-market with bait, fishing equipment, clothing and all kinds of other goods. He opens especially early for me...well for me and others," he laughed with a smile in his voice. "Marty is the person to ask what's biting or what bait to use, etc. If you order a bag lunch it's waiting for you in the morning. After all, if the fish are biting, who wants to stop for lunch," he finished.

If the fishermen were lucky, they would go to Marty's and have their photo taken with their catch. If they don't want to cook them themselves, they either sell them to Marty or clean them and freeze them to take back home after their holiday. Some of the good ole boys come every year.

The evening is over and the sun is down and all is right with the world. Elaine is in her cabin, Lou in hers. Hopefully, they will have a good night's rest because there's a busy day waiting for them in town that might prove dangerous. Grant's Pass, Oregon, is known as a great place and no one would even think of intrigue in this lovely place.

# Chapter 7

Lou and Elaine received a message from the front desk that breakfast would be served in the dining area from 5:00 a.m. until 10:00 a.m. Elaine was just returning from her run when she got her message and Lou was talking to her handler with her latest updates. They decided to meet for breakfast at the restaurant.

The message Lou received in her package indicated the local law enforcement was having trouble with a young man who was stealing ladies' handbags early in the day. His description and M.O. was medium build and he went looking for affluent women shopping alone always near a shop with an alley next to it for an easy escape. Sometimes he would hang around local cafes where they could get coffee and rest their feet. When the victim came out, he made sure she was alone. The young man waited until she would come out of the cafe and start to walk. He always approached from behind and grabbed the lady around the neck or torso while trying to steal her handbag. TIA wants Lou to try to find this guy before he harms anyone else. Lou was going shopping anyway so they want her to keep an eye out for him; dress for the occasion but do not take chances.

In the morning Lou and Elaine met at the dining area and were seated opposite each other at the same table. Each waited for the waitress to show them today's breakfast menu. The waitress went around the table and took their orders. Already on the table was orange juice, coffee, tea, and water for them while they waited for their food. Most of the people at the table were either going into town for boating, swimming, biking, or just going for a hike around the grounds and hitting the small shops in the lodge.

Lou came out of her cabin wearing a western style casual elegant outfit. Elaine knew she was given something to check out by TIA while on her trip to town. One look from anyone and you would know she had money. Lou was in her designer casual blouse, tight fitting jeans with matching boots, and saddle bag style handbag. Elaine knew Lou had goodies in that handbag for protection...so something is definitely going on.

The girls met at the Rover and headed for town. Lou showed Elaine where to drop her off, which was about a block from the shops she had to visit. It was agreed that they were to meet at the Rover when both were given the address where it was to be parked.

Lou was walking down the street and window shopping and at the same time working on catching this man. Lou received a message and TIA told her the last robbery was yesterday and it seems the perpetrator moved to larger things. This time he did it in the middle of town and had kidnapped the woman. The police found her dead body washed up on the banks of the river. Her purse was missing and there were bruises in the same area as the other women that were robbed while shopping. The police believe it is the same man, same M.O., with the exception now it was murder.

Lou was remembering what Nanny Brown drilled into her when was still young. Nanny would say what to do when, "you see a 'bad man' and he tries to touch you or harm you in any way." Lou was looking in the cafe window and she had come a long way since Nanny Browns' wise advice on safety.

Lou saw the reflection of the tourists walking and enjoying the sights of downtown and there were many young men all over the place. There was one young man that was medium height and just standing by the bench. This seemed odd as he was not doing anything. *This could be the perp*, she thought. So,Lou walked slowly along the front of the cafe. Near the window she saw him start walking behind her. Lou let TIA know she thought the perp was following her and they were coming close to a store where there was an alley next to it. Sure enough when they were out of sight of the store window but not to the alley she got the feeling he was walking faster trying to catch up with her.

He rushed Lou from behind. She was prepared for his next move. He put his left arm around her neck and was tugging at her purse that she had over her shoulder. Lou immediately grabbed his left arm with her right hand. Lou was wearing one of her goodies, which was a ring that by pressing her thumb against the back of the ring caused a flame that immediately caused the hair on his arm and shirt to catch fire and at the same time gave a hard stomp on his foot with her boot. This caused him to release his choke hold. That was the last thing he had expected Lou to do. The perp was more concerned with his pain, which allowed Lou time to turn around and finish him with an upper cut to his nose. She used such force it broke his nose and he immediately collapsed.

Lou pulled him into the alley and cuffed his hands and feet to large pipes that came down from the roof of the store. Before he could regain consciousness, Lou got her lip gloss out of her handbag and used it on his lips. This great goodie causes any person that comes in contact with it to pass out for at least twenty minutes. *When he wakes up he won't remember anything*, she thought.

Lou called TIA and they will take it from here. She was told to put the company's business card in his pocket with a note that the police should be called and the law enforcement are to contact TIA as this is at least one of the perps robbing women on their streets. Lou stepped back on the sidewalks and proceeded to do her shopping and wait for Elaine to contact her.

Elaine stopped for gas at the specified gas station where she filled up the tank. While paying the manager, she asked to have the attendant check the oil, gas, and tire pressure. The man that came to assist her said, "Would you like your windshield washed?"

Her reply was, "No thanks, I'm in a hurry." He then slipped her a message as she tipped him.

Elaine put the message in her zippered pocket and got back in the car. She would read the message later. Elaine decided to look around town. She got out of the Rover, pushing a button on the dash letting TIA know where the car was parked, allowing them to watch so no one could tamper with the car. The new system installed had an automatic camera which showed everything around the immediate area. Elaine noticed the bracelet on her wrist was flashing, which meant there was an undercover agent and/or a TIA agent within their area of concern. Both Lou and Elaine had been notified. They kept on doing what they were doing for another fifteen minutes when they received notification of where to go to get the Rover as it had been moved.

Elaine was given instructions and the route she was to take to get to a safe area; and if the coast was clear, her bracelet color would return to normal. She was then to proceed to parking area and to the specified parking spot. The dash was flashing and the message was to keep going two blocks, turn right, and right again until the flashing stopped. There was something unknown in the area. Elaine continued on to the correct address number of where the car was parked. She got out of the Rover and walked to an area which protected her from all sides, hiding until her bracelet returned to the all-clear. That meant she could return to the Rover and Lou would be inside.

Lou was given instructions on what streets she was to take to the parked Rover. Lou will be monitored by TIA and her bracelet will turn a color if she is clear. The Rover will automatically unlock if the coast is clear or stay locked until the danger has passed. She is to keep walking if the door is locked. Fortunately, Lou was able to get into the car and shortly after Elaine got in and the dash flashed all clear.

"I wonder which of us was tailed?" Lou said, still a bit shaken.

"Got me! I had to do some evasive driving for a few minutes. It seemed the longest five minutes of my life," Elaine replied.

Lou said, "I guess we will never know as it is not like TIA to give us any information."

They returned straight to the bed and breakfast, parked, and went to the pub. Each entered from a different door. Elaine motioned to Lou to join her if she wasn't waiting for someone. Lou motioned with a smile—she would be happy to join her and mentioned she only had stopped in for an afternoon social drink. The bartender served them their drinks, along with a bowl of peanuts. They both enjoyed the drink and finally calmed down.

Just before they were to order another drink, they both received a message from TIA. They were to go to their cabins and wait until they heard from their handlers. With a strange look in their eyes, they signed their cabin numbers on the bar tab and left one at a time.

# Chapter 8

Elaine entered her cabin and her phone rang. It was TIA. She answered on the second ring and a familiar voice by the name of Bill said, "Come on! Come on!"

Elaine laughed and said, "Hi Bill, what is the latest news? I was a little distracted with the division in the route to park in town earlier."

Bill said, "We were notified that there was another body of a young woman found in the local area. I want you to go to the alley behind Marty's and knock once and then three times fast at the back door. When answered, say it is Elaine at Cabin 13 and not your real cabin number. He is expecting you. You will pick up a package informing you of all the bodies that have been found on or in the water along the coast. Examine every detail of all the women's profiles and see if you can come up with what they may have in common. Need I tell you this is needed urgently? We know it is not the person you are looking for; however, it looks like this young woman was taken in Arizona. Somehow, we do feel it is connected to your case." And he hung up.

Elaine took her flashlight in hand and went to Marty's place and there was a light on over the back door. She knocked once, then three times fast. Marty said, "Who is it?"

"Elaine in Cabin 13."

With that he opened the door and proceeded to turn off the light. He handed the package to her and looked around to make sure there was no one around.

She nodded and then walked around the corner of the building. Then she turned on the flashlight and walked back to her cabin.

It took four hours to thoroughly check out the murders. The women were not all killed the same way and no sign of molestation according to the final autopsy. However, in each case there was one item found on each person or on their clothes, which was some type of jewelry and may or may not prove helpful, as most women wear some sort of jewelry such as a ring, bracelet, or necklace. Elaine surmised it was something to note, as it meant, whomever murdered these women didn't take all their identification or just overlooked it.

I think it is a long stretch to assume robbery, however, it felt like the jewelry was left on purpose or a gift the abdicator gave the women. Without further knowledge of each women's personal information, it is hard to come to a firm conclusion. She will have to have TIA check out the personal information of every individual body.

Elaine contacted Bill and he turned on the scrambler so she could forward the results of her findings and answer any questions she may have. All she could do now was wait for what they came up with. She closed the message and after brushing her teeth and a warm shower went to bed.

After Lou went to her cabin, she showered and did a few personal evening routines: facial cleansing, applied face and body lotion, dental hygiene, and drank her usual tall glass of water. She snuggled into bed for what she thought would be a long night's sleep. After two hours of solid sleep, Lou was startled by the phone beeping. She reached over and found she had received a message from her handler. She called back and a voice answered immediately:

"Sorry to wake you, but this cannot wait. Your case has had a turn of events. Diane Lane left another vague message saying her hunch is proving fruitful...she is safe but has found out there is more happening in this tourist area surrounding ocean shores. Nothing more was mentioned and we fear she may be over her head. Not that she can't handle most situations, but we do not want any of our team to take chances. Keep an eye on your goodies in case you receive an, 'I am in danger signal.'

"If you do, tell Elaine no stops barred and full-speed ahead. If Diane's ESP is working overtime, there needs to be someone else around to keep track of her lodging and find out what her cover is so we can have more control over what it is she thinks she has discovered. Lou, since you know Diane and have had her work with you, maybe you can at least make her go directly to the agency in Ocean Shores. As talented as Diane is, sometimes she forgets about teamwork and acts like a bloodhound running rogue.

"When Elaine finishes her case, she will be able to assist you without Diane Lane knowing that she is even in Ocean Shores. Let us know when you arrive at Copalis Beach cottage and are settled in. There will be a car for you in the garage and Elaine can retain the Rover.

"Lou, there is an office in Ocean Shores. It is a small commercial building on the road just outside of the pillars/arches that lead into Ocean Shores main street. They are familiar with the things that go on all over the area and not just Ocean Shores. For a small office, this agency has top secret information and high-clearance employees. Feel free to talk to Rosie and show her your ID card. Just don't let on your reason for being in the area is other than vacation and to enjoy the Fourth of July on the beach.

"Casually ask Rosie if she knows if there is any other personnel from the agency also vacationing locally. Maybe you know them and could let them know you are in town. You could meet with them and have a bite to eat, etc. In fact, if you could have their names and contact address while in town, you will certainly try and see them.

"If Diane Lane is there she would have checked in at the agency because as you know it is one of the first rules any agent learns. She will probably have shown Rosie her ID card."

After hanging up, Lou tried to go back to sleep. She was restless thinking about Diane and what problem she thought she might have stumbled onto. She dosed fitfully close to 5:00 a.m. In the morning, Lou got up. She showered, did her usual rubdown with lotion and face cream and dressed in her casual clothes for the long drive that was ahead of her. The breakfast call came in from the dining room and she was ready and hungry. Lou walked to the lodge and went in.

Elaine, as usual had been on her run, showered, dressed and arrived early for juice and coffee. She was seated at a small table as most of the visitors were up and out trying their luck at fishing. Lou came walking in smiling and looked fresh as a daisy. She was seated with Elaine and the waitress asked if they needed to be introduced? They thanked her and said they had been introduced last evening. "Good, do you want a menu or do you know what you would like?"

Lou who always sips her coffee and suggests waiting a few minutes before ordering said with a smile in her voice, "I think

I would like a couple of the chefs sourdough pancakes, two sunny side up eggs, and whatever meat the chef thinks I would enjoy."

Elaine was surprised at Lou's appetite. Elaine looked at the waitress with a smile, as she saw an amazed look on her face, "I will have the same."

Lou drank fresh orange juice and not waiting for the waitress to return, filled both their coffee cups. Elaine said happily, "Lou, it almost seems you are getting the hang of just relaxing and learning to go with the flow. You haven't relaxed like this since you went on your first picnic."

Lou answered, "I just wanted to savor the last morning we will be here. I am having a good time and playing darts with the good ole-boys. Last evening reminded me of being in the local pub in Canada with Mom, Dad, and Nanny. Remember, I learned how to throw darts while we were on that trip?" *Too bad we must leave*, she thought.

Elaine said, "You must have been contacted last evening and given instructions to travel?"

Lou said, "Yes, I was on the phone forever. Seems duty calls both of us. I am glad you are driving. I didn't rest well after my phone conference and will probably take a nap. I think we should fill our supply of hot coffee so we don't have to stop frequently."

Elaine said, "We can order sandwiches and fill our thermos bottles and separately notify the office we are checking out."

Elaine went to the lodge first and notified them she was checking out of her cabin. She thanked them for a great stay and she hoped to see them again soon.

## Chapter 9

Lou was sitting in the Rover waiting for Elaine to return with the coffee and sandwiches, which she placed near the front seat for easy access while they loaded the Rover.

With the car loaded, they were ready to head on their way. Elaine hesitated at Marty's place and told Lou to wait a minute. "I need to thank Marty for the kindness he extended me for the hot coffee/water he gave me when I went on my early morning runs." What she really wanted, was to see if Marty had received any other packages for her before she headed on her vacation.

Marty ensured her there were no further packages received for her. "Enjoy the rest of your trip, as no news he hoped was good news. We certainly enjoyed your staying at our lodge. It has been a pleasant change for the ole boys at the pub. God speed, Elaine."

She jumped into the Rover and the safety belts automatically fastened. A voice from TIA came from the dash, "Stay safe!"

They drove out of town and both Elaine and Lou were watching all their bells and whistles on their goodies as well as the area around the car and sidewalks. They knew they needed to be aware of everything and everyone.

Elaine received a message. She put in her earplugs and listened to the message. The voice stated, "You should drive carefully and at the same time, be safe. You have the go ahead to drive over the speed limit, as the authorities are aware of your Rover and your urgency. When necessary, if you have to make a stop, your dash will flash and give you a location of the safest gas station. Always gas up, even if you only need a small amount of gas so that we have a paper trail besides our constant transmitter of your whereabouts. You should avoid downtown Portland at all cost, as it is overrun with the homeless and derelicts. Gas up in Aberdeen where it is safer. Aberdeen is like a county seat for the surrounding areas and cities. If you ever need information about a particular area of Washington State, inquire within the visitors' station. The head woman in charge at the station...is in the know."

Lou was glancing out of the car window noticing how well the road signage in this state designated curves and hills, helping to reminded you to always keep right if traveling slow. Even the trucks seem to obey signage.

Thank goodness they got coffee and sandwiches before they left so they did not have to stop anywhere. They found a rest area sign and asked Rover if it was safe. Amazingly, it turned out to be one of their controlled areas to stop. They both made a pit stop: one stayed at the Rover until the other returned. They had their goodies on alert in case they were, for whatever reason, stopped by anyone...TIA was alerted and TIA personnel would be on top of it.

With Lou or Elaine's skills, they could handle any situation, as they were top of their class in self-defense among other techniques. After they both returned to the Rover, they grabbed a sandwich and poured the coffee.

They talked as they ate and wondered what the cottage would look like. The agent that owned the cottage said we should stop at the Purple Pub, if for no other reason they were famous in the area. The Purple Pub was known for their relaxing atmosphere, local drinks, and great pub food. All the locals frequented it to play a game of friendly darts, shuffleboard, or pool.

Elaine collected the trash and threw it in the recycling containers provided. As they were headed out, Elaine wondered how long before the turn-off was to downtown Portland, which they might avoid.

They had been driving a long time when a light started flashing letting them know a turn they were to take was coming up on the right. Elaine took the turn and mentioned to Lou it was the long way around the town, but short if you looked at the alternative driving downtown Portland. "We sure don't want to get involved in the unknown," said Elaine.

They continued to drive what seemed like forever and it was starting to get dark. "I guess we should check in with TIA and find where it is alright to stop and have a good meal," said Lou.

TIA came on the dash and told them, "In 5.2 miles on the right hand-side, you will see a road sign indicating there is a 1950s diner. Believe it or not, they have great food, top service and desserts fit for a queen." They pulled into the parking area right in front of the steps. The Rover was safe as long as Elaine activated all the gadgets.

The hostess asked, "Two for dinner?" Elaine wondered, *Why is it...when seeing there is no one in sight, does the person that leads us to our seats always ask that question? I want to reply to them, "Yes, unless you have two great looking, rich men waiting for us." But then we already have our share of those, so what would be the point.*

Elaine said to Lou quietly, "I wonder if they have a good filet mignon, medium rare with fried buttered mushrooms, fresh dinner salad, and a twice baked potato. Maybe dessert, if it is homemade. It doesn't hurt to ask."

Lou looked over at Elaine and winked and said she would try the same thing. The 1950s dressed waitress with a pencil and pad took their order and asked what they wanted to drink. Elaine told Lou to get a good glass of Cabernet wine and she would, if they have it, get a green tea. Lou ordered the house wine. The waitress delivered the best pot of green tea Elaine had had in a long time. The waitress looked at Lou and stated she took it upon herself to bring her a wine she was sure to really enjoy. Lou said, "Thank you for the thoughtfulness."

The only thing like a 1950s diner was the cool name, cloth napkins, drinks to their liking, best filet mignon in months, and the salad served last. Lou said, "Can you imagine serving salad last like Paris, remember Elaine?"

"I'll say," Elaine said, and I can't wait to see what the dessert list will entail."

They both ate almost everything on their plate and spoke softly again to each other, "I have to save room for dessert."

Lou mentioned she would have to go on a veggie diet when she returned home. The way she had been eating on their trip might warrant drastic measures. Elaine suggested she just put on her running shoes and go running with her every chance she gets. Lou looked at Elaine with the most incredulous eyes and said, "Are you kidding? Look they have crème brulée and baked Alaska." They settled on crème brulée.

They paid the tab with the credit card Lou received in her package. Elaine thought, *They always give Lou whatever she wants when it comes to shopping, including food.* She suggested that they get a refill on coffee to go...heaven only knows what they charge for coffee to go?

They went to the Rover and flashed their ankle bracelet side by side as they went around the car. Nothing came up on their goodies so they unlocked the doors and got in. "And away we go!" said Lou. She was enjoying this vacation more than Elaine thought she would. That's when Elaine knew the case Lou was on must be in Ocean Shores. Elaine and Lou were always on the same wave-length as most twins are, so Elaine wasn't really guessing.

Lou had her seat in nap position, her sunglasses on, and with a smile said, "Onward and up-wards, Jeeves. A new journey awaits beyond the horizon."

Elaine said, "As you wish miss."

She drove faster than usual and pushed on the button that checks all around the sides so they would not get into an accident or attract the highway patrol. They had already lost too much time at the 1950s diner.

The curves and hills were a thrill when they traveled so fast. It seemed like the trucks that crowded the two right lanes all moved over like the parting of the seas. TIA must really have notified all the powers that be to clear the way.

Elaine wondered what new personal information they came up with on all the women that were found deceased. She certainly was ready to review the individual records to see if they had anything she could possible pick up that would give her a clue as to how, where, and when the killer would lure his next victim.

Elaine looked over at Lou who was still taking a nap. Her eye glanced at the dash to see how fast she was going and then the flashing started and a message came up: "Confidential! ear plugs and contact Bill." She did as she was told. "Come on! Come on!" she heard.

Elaine softly spoke, "What has happened to wake you up at this time of night?"

Bill excitedly told her they received the information she requested. "Stop at the indicated station for gas...Sam The Man, as he is known to be called, is the person to ask for when you go to pay. He will have a package for you."

Elaine pulled into the gas station, filled up and went in search of Sam The Man. Sam The Man asked, "Would like a copy of today's paper?"

Elaine said, "Sure, go ahead and charge me for it."

Elaine got back in the car and was on the road again, fast. Lou woke up, saw the paper and said to Elaine, "Thanks for the newspaper, that was very thoughtful Elaine."

Elaine answered, "You can thank Sam The Man. He has something in it for me, hopefully an envelope?"

Lou opened the newspaper and retrieved the envelope, which she placed next to Elaine in between the seat and console. Lou said, "I'll read the newspaper and see if something interesting pops out. . . Oh, my god! Here's something we should know. I wonder why TIA didn't tell us? The headline says and I quote: 'Who done it?' Then adds, 'Several unknown women have been found brutally murdered along the west coast, with the latest last evening near the borders of Oregon and the state of Washington.'"

"Heavens girl!" Lou said, "We picked the wrong time to travel this way."

Elaine shook her head in agreement. Not wanting to let Lou know that it might be the case that she is now working on. In the envelope, she hopes she'll find some clues to help catch this serial killer.

The dash flashed fast and Lou told Elaine that it states you are to continue traveling the way you have been fast, fast, and faster. Lou had been taking catnaps and wasn't really paying attention. "What do you think?" said Lou, "Do we keep driving fast and arrive earlier in Copalis Beach, Washington?"

Elaine stated, "Yes! We just by-passed downtown Portland. We are almost to Aberdeen where I would like to stop at Walmart for a few essentials for the cottage just in case we have a difficult time finding things."

Lou agreed. By the time they reached Copalis Beach, everything would be closed.

# Chapter 10

Just before arriving in Aberdeen, the dash started to flash. There was a message for Elaine and she should put her ear plugs in: "Confidential."

Elaine put the ear plugs in and immediately heard, "Come on! Come on!" She said, "Hi Bill, what is the latest?"

He replied, "You will have a stop to make at the address I'm sending now. It's a drive-thru coffee shack. Say you have a special request for Mike's sister. She will have a package for you if you say, 'one regular black coffee and one grande iced mocha frappuccino.'

"Up the road, five miles on the right, will be a truck stop. You can peruse the paperwork from Sam The Man. Call back and let me know if you need more information. Also, have you come up with what you think the profile of the killer might be? We understand due to your driving, it will only be preliminary.

"The local cities need help now, as they don't have the qualifications for finding criminal profilers without more input. We can't tell them how we come up with the suggested profile, at this time, but just a suggestion of the type man or woman they should be looking for."

Elaine said, "Ten four, over and out." She pressed the ignition key and drove on.

She drove into Aberdeen and stopped in the Walmart parking lot. Elaine asked Lou to inform TIA they were in the Walmart parking lot and that she was staying in the Rover while Elaine purchased some groceries. They will secure the area and keep the car under surveillance. Elaine came back and decided they should top off their gas.

They pulled into the nearest gas station. As they pulled up to the pumps, the parking lot suddenly filled up with police cars, sirens wailing and lights flashing. Elaine shouted above the noise to the gas attendant, "What's going on?"

The gas station attendant said, "The police have surrounded a crazy man brandishing a weapon. Not sure what his problem is though?"

The gas attendant apologized profusely and told Elaine that he would have to close the pumps until the crisis was over. Elaine totally understood his reasoning. She said thanks and continued their drive out of town. They were glad they weren't witnesses to what had transpired; they didn't need any delays at this point in their travels. They quickly headed for the highway and again the dash flashed.

This time Lou was requested to put in her ear plugs. Lou was instructed to stay overnight with Elaine and not proceed to Copalis Beach tonight. Elaine was to call Bill.

A message came for Elaine before Lou had a chance to tell her. Lou knew there must be something very important happening. Elaine was told they were checking in Hoquiam, Washington, and where they could stay. By the time they arrived in Hoquiam, they would have the name of a secure place to stay. There would be a package at the reservation desk for her. They were to get a two room accommodation. Elaine was to give them her ID and credit card and tell them they would like the rooms for two nights— that parking the Rover outside Elaine's room is a must. The Rover would indicate to the appropriate staff who they were in order to receive the package!

The dash flashed with the name of the lodging: Econo Lodge Inn and Suites, just off the highway, Exit 22. Further instructions in package. Read it and you take it from there.

# Chapter 11

In the meantime, because of the dangers happening all at once on the cases Elaine and Lou were on, TIA sent in undercover agents. These agents would change their identity, looks and secure employment where needed, which would be prearranged by TIA. Surprise! Surprise! As for the agents that in their hay day were noted for being able to speak and look completely different, even TIA could not recognize them, as they became none other than Harry and Ms. Brown from Lou and Elaine's estate in California. One might say they could have been actors if they wanted.

Harry and Ms. Brown were requested and had to immediately go to Santa Monica airport and retrieve a package at the airport office. In the package they were given instructions. They were to change their appearance and make it good enough to fool Elaine, Lou, and Diane Lane.

The message: "You will fly to Aberdeen and pick up a sports car for Lou. It will contain all the bells and whistles she will require. Drive it to the address in Copalis Beach and park it in the garage. You are to stay at the Indian casino.

"When you have arrived at the cottage in Copalis Beach, call the casino and give them the address of where to pick you up for your stay. You will have your confirmation number. After you check in, you are to go to your suite and disguise yourselves.

"Ms. Brown, you will be employed at Ace Hardware in Ocean Shores. Harry, you will be a waiter in the restaurant in the casino. Accept the hours they give you. This is probably the most important test of your lives when it comes to disguises. Lou and Elaine will eat at the restaurant and go to the hardware store, so you will be running into them often. The agents in that local area are Lou, Elaine, and Diane Lane. Diane's photo is in your package."

Upon their arrival, they went to the office at the casino and got their suite. Everything was complete as directed and they would never be seen again by anyone in the casino as anyone other than the waiter and Ace Hardware employee.

Elaine and Lou arrived at the Econo Lodge and Suites. Elaine went in and received her package after giving the required information.

They went to their individual rooms where Elaine opened the package. Lou's phone rang and as she was getting her information, Elaine was reading her instructions. It seems TIA received word that another body was just found in the town of Hoquiam. Elaine was to go to the scene of the crime and check in with the highway patrol. It was the first time Elaine was in the area at the time a body was found and as a criminal profiler she would be invaluable.

The highway patrol was waiting eagerly for her arrival. They secured the area and kept everyone away so Elaine could see how the killer left the body. They did, however, get a description of a car leaving the area where the body was found.

"What have you got for me?" Elaine asked.

The detective said, "We have a person that thinks she can identify the car that was in the area. Don't know if it means anything, but we held her here pending your arrival. Also, in the sand there is a tire tread. We photographed it and also took an impression."

Elaine had them send her a copy of the photo and asked to speak to the witness that saw the car: she was about thirty-five and familiar with automobiles as she worked for a car dealership in the sales department. Elaine introduced herself to the witness. She noticed she was a well-dressed salesperson in an Ann Taylor dark navy suit, which was accented by an orange silk blouse with just enough exposure to entice prospective buyers (if you get my drift). She was well spoken, precise and very knowledgeable in her description. She said, "It was a Caucasian male, brown hair, young, say about twenty-five or so. He was driving a 2022 Chevrolet Malibu LT sedan, four door, turbocharged, two hundred fifty horsepower four-cylinder engine, tan in color. I didn't get the license plate number, but it came from Arizona."

Elaine thanked her and had the highway patrol officer take her phone number and other information. If she needed to speak with her again, they would have her information on file.

Elaine walked away with her phone in her hand and contacted Bill: "I will be sending you the tire tread photo and the information the woman gave us on the vehicle. One of the most important bits of information was that the car came from Arizona. That, along with the make and model, color being tan, and tire tread photo should narrow down the search for suspects. I will give you more information when I have more insight into the killer's profile."

Bill said, "If I have the correct facts, so far we have narrowed it to possibly a Caucasian male, brown hair, twenty-five or so, plus the color and make of the car with a license plate from Arizona."

Elaine added, "We will narrow it down further Bill, once we have the results of the coroner's inquest, which might give us more details of what happened to the body, etc."

With Elaine's criminal profiling enhanced by the coroner's biopsy and what she might find on the woman's clothing, she might just find this bastard.

# Chapter 12

The coroner has his offices in a medium sized home. Office, lab and lodging all in one. Hoquiam is a very small city so the highway patrol and town are very lucky to have one in their area. Elaine entered the offices and was taken to the lab where she found a senior coroner dressed in white scrubs. In many cases, it is advantageous to have a senior more knowledgeable doctor who has handled many different types of autopsies. He is semi-retired with a receding hairline and sporting horn-rimmed glasses. He had a lovely smile and a spring in his step and spoke with authority. He held out his hand and in a robust voice introduced himself: "Just call me Doc, everyone in town does...and you are?"

"I'm Elaine, a criminal profiler sent to see if I can come up with any additional information along with what you may find in your examination of the woman."

Elaine added, "Just between you and me, we might have a serial killer on our hands. Let's hope this is going to be the last body we find and because of your experience in such matters you just might be the instrument of his capture."

There was silence for a short time as Elaine watched Doc continue with his procedures. A pause came and Elaine asked Doc if she could see the items given him from the crime scene to check out. Doc replied, "Check today's date on the packages marked 'Jane Doe'. Please wear gloves before you touch anything. I'm still doing my preliminary autopsy as requested, so you can keep going on your preliminary profiling. Hopefully, you'll find articles that will help in finding out the identification of this poor lady."

One of the first things she looked for was jewelry to see if it was a copycat murder or related to all the other bodies found along the coast. If there is, they may have something more to go on immediately.

A highway patrol officer came into the lab with urgent findings around the area where Jane Doe was found. Elaine thanked him for bringing the latest bits of forensic information.

Elaine put down the envelope and continued to examine the jacket where she found a brooch on the left-side lapel. Upon inspection of the jacket pockets, was a neatly folded invoice/order receipt with itemized items purchased from the local office supply company. The invoice/order form was signed by a Pete somebody. The last name was not legible. Thank goodness the company name was on the invoice: Hoquiam Office Supply Company. *What a break,* she thought.

Elaine put down the jacket and opened the envelope the highway patrol officer delivered and sat down to read a total list of things found at the sight of where Jane Doe was murdered. She went through the list to see if there was anything found after she left the murder sight. There were bone fragments on the ground where the body was found. Then, a partial footprint with a pointed toe, as well as blood drops on the ground under the body of Jane Doe.

Elaine whispered to herself, "Well, this combined with what I have found may really prove to be what will expedite this case."

She told Doc she was going to go check some things that might lead to the identity of Jane Doe. She thought to herself who the killer might be.

Elaine went to the parking lot and as she got into the Rover, she saw a message from Lou. She was hoping Elaine could take a break and grab something to eat. Elaine hadn't realized that it was past mealtime. Lou suggested she meet her at the lodge cafe for, hopefully, some good food.

Lou was waiting outside the cafe and they both went in. It was a quaint place with tablecloths, checkered window curtains, soft seats, and smelled like a mother's kitchen. A sandwich plate piled high with french fries and salad passed by and looked so good. The aroma of coffee and homemade pies made their mouths water.

The waitress came to take their order. Her name tag bore the name "Bess." She wore a white apron, starched with pockets that held straws and napkins. With a pencil behind her ear and an order pad in her hand she asked, "What'll it be ladies?"

"What is the special of the day?" Lou asked.

Bess laughed and said, "Chili, but then it is always the special of the day."

"We will have a menu please," Elaine said.

They checked out the menu and decided to order a chicken breast sandwich on rye, french fries, salad greens with balsamic vinaigrette dressing, and coffee.

Bess shouted to a cutout in the wall leading to the kitchen, "Two chicks on rye with all of the fixings. Make it fast, we have some hungry young ladies here."
"I'll do my best!" said someone in the kitchen.

"Thanks Joe!" Bess replied.

Steaming hot coffee in large mugs came to Lou and Elaine's rescue. The sandwiches were ready in a timely fashion. "Let me know if you ladies need anything else?" Bess said as she refilled their coffee cups.

Elaine expressed that the food was very yummy. The salad was large and fresh and the chicken sandwich was very tasty.

Elaine mentioned she had some calls to make to inquire about some important facts she had received from the coroner and the police before she could continue with her profiling. Elaine said, "Where can I take you Lou?"

Lou said, "I'll go back to the hotel room as I'm expecting a call. We can meet up again later for dinner."

Elaine said, "That's a good idea. I'll contact you after I get the required information I need, that I hope will complete my case.

Elaine pulled into the parking lot of Hoquiam Office Supply Company. As she went into the lobby, she heard a voice say, "Please have a seat and I'll be with you in a moment." It was a clean lobby with black chairs, a small end table, and a real plant. A young woman came in from the inside office area. She motioned for Elaine to come up to the front reception desk.

Elaine smiled and said, "Hello!" She signed into the visitors book the receptionist pointed to.

"Are you here to deliver something, sell something or talk to someone," the receptionist enquired, as a smile came over her face.

Elaine laughed and said, "I need to speak to the manager about a private business matter."

"That would be Ms. Robertson, who is not in the building at the moment. Mr. Carlson, our assistant manager, is available," the receptionist offered.

With that, Elaine said, "My name is Elaine and that would be nice as I am on a tight schedule."
The girl pressed the intercom button and asked Mr. Carlson to please come to the reception area. "He will be here shortly as his office is in the back of the building," she said.

Elaine sat down and waited. Five minutes passed and in walked a handsome middle-aged man. His voice and demeanor was everything you would want in management.

Elaine introduced herself and gave him her case business card. The expression on his face was very expressive and one could tell he had never seen a card from a criminal forensic profiler before.

Mr. Carlson said, "This is an office supply company who handles both wholesale and retail merchandise. Are you sure you have the right place?"

Elaine told him that what she needed to discuss with him was private business and for his ears only.

Mr. Carlson suggested they go to his office. He allowed her to enter the reception area and then through the office area to the back of the building.

Elaine noticed there were several cubicles with men and women taking orders and processing paperwork. She wondered which lady did not return from lunch.

Mr. Carlson ushered Elaine into his office and shut the door. "Now what is all this cloak and dagger business you have to discuss?"

"Mr. Carlson, for now I would like this to be between us. It has not been made public as of yet, but it will be later in the day. There has been a murder of a woman that had an invoice/order form in her pocket that had your companies name on it. At this time, I can't go into detail of what happened to her. I am here to see if you can tell me who would have that specific order form in her pocket." She gave him the number that was on the form and requested he not alarm anyone. "Just request a copy of that form and clarify the full signature of the vendor—a Pete somebody. Please ask the person to verify who took the order and which vendor ordered it."

Mr. Carlson picked up the phone and pressed the button of the office manager. "Jack!" He said, "There was an order placed this morning." He gave him the form number and asked who placed it. "While you are at it Jack you might as well give me the salesman's full name and companies phone number. Nothing's wrong, but you know me, Jack, when I come across something not legible I wonder why. My bad!" he said and hung up.

Mr. Carlson said, "If I asked Jack to hurry, it might start him wondering and ask questions that at this time I can't answer and that would lead to more questions. Jack always knows when I ask a question, I want an immediate response."

I checked my watch to see how long it would take Jack to get the information Mr. Carlson requested. Five minutes went by and there was a knock at the door and Mr. Carlson said, "Come in Jack."

Jack handed him a copy of the form with a paper attached with the name and phone number of the vendor. "The order was placed by Ms. Robertson just before she left for lunch. Is there anything else you need?" Jack asked.

Elaine mentioned softly to Mr. Carlson that she would like to know where Ms. Robertson went to lunch. Jack overheard her and quickly replied, "Betty might know. I'll send her in to see you." Elaine asked Mr. Carlson to let her ask the questions.

Please explain that I am a friend of Ms. Robertson and would like to inquire about Ms. Robertson's lunch plans and what she had on for this afternoon.

Betty knocked at Mr. Carlson's door and was asked to come in. As Elaine requested, he introduced her to Betty. Mr. Carlson said it was alright for Betty to help her in her quest to locate Ms. Robertson.

Elaine smiled and told Betty she was in town for a short time and was going to invite Ms. Robertson to lunch. Betty said, "Oh, you are too late because she went to lunch with Pete. I was surprised she said okay, as she has always turned him down before because she said she thought him to be kinda creepy. With his cowboy boots, suit, squeaky like voice and all, I guess she just wanted to tell him not to bother asking her to lunch anymore, but everyone was listening to what she would say. Before she could answer Pete, he said he had reservations at the best restaurant in town. I know Ms. Robertson knew that if she refused Pete, he would throw a fit."

Elaine asked, "What place did Pete mention?"

Betty replied, "It's a new upscale restaurant on the beach called Francisco's By The Beach. It just opened recently. I would have gone if Pete asked me because it's really supposed to be a classy place. It's funny she isn't back, as she usually never takes more

*Del Uvon Bates*

than a couple of hours at the most for lunch unless she tells me differently."

When Elaine heard that, the hair in the back of her neck stood on end. She now knew it was a possibility that Jane Doe was Ms. Robertson. Elaine looked at Mr. Carlson and indicated she was finished talking to Betty.

Mr. Carlson said, "Thank you Betty for taking time to talk to Elaine. I know your time is valuable."

Betty smiled and said, "No problem Mr. Carlson, and if I can be of help in the future please count on me."

When Betty shut the door, Elaine looked at Mr. Carlson, and in a very serious voice asked if he could supply her with a photo of Ms. Robertson.

"Oh sure!" he said as he picked up a promotional article about the company. Ms. Robertson was featured on the front page of the magazine. The article stating Ms. Robertson as the owner and general manager of the up-and-coming Hoquaim Office Supply Company this side of Aberdeen, Washington.

Elaine quickly glanced at the picture of her. There was no question in her mind that it was Ms. Robertson. Elaine stood up and asked if she could have the magazine. Mr. Carlson said, "Yes, of course as they had many more."

Elaine thanked him and said that he'd be hearing from her or the highway patrol soon. "Please do not discuss this with anyone for now. She must be identified first." With that she left the office.

Now Elaine's work begins in full force. She must first get as much information from Francisco's By The Beach restaurant and gather evidence and/or interview persons that served Ms. Robertson and Pete. She hoped she was not too late to talk to the waiter/waitress that took care of them. But first Elaine must inform TIA.

# Chapter 13

Elaine entered Francisco's where she encountered a maître d'. As one might expect, there stood a handsome self-assured gentleman around forty-five or so in age; lots of black hair with just the right number of gray accents. It was a busy time of the day; he probably received extra pocket money on the side for a "now" reservation from walk-in patrons. Both men and women would enjoy his attention and would be generous with their tip so they would be remembered. His memory of faces and names is certainly exceptional!

He approached Elaine and she handed him her business card. The name tag indicated his name was Antonio. He held out his hand as though they were great friends. She held out her hand and said, "Hello Antonio, do you have a few moments so we can privately chat?"

With a smile and sparkle in his eyes he called over someone to take the reservation desk while he took a break. He looked for her name on the business card...Elaine. "So, what can I do for you? I see you are affiliated in some way with the local police?"

Antonio guided her to a small table where they could talk privately. Before she could speak, he motioned to a nearby waiter and asked me what Elaine would like to drink. She said, "A cup of hot coffee with a touch of cream."

Antonio said, "Make it two."

Elaine smiled and said to Antonio, "I know at your restaurant no one needs to ask for 'hot' coffee; however, I've been traveling and one must ask for the coffee to be hot or it may come lukewarm."

"Been there, done that, so many times myself, when I was traveling in Europe," Antonio said.

Elaine smiled and asked, "What kind of job had you traveling in Europe?"

With a smile Antonio said, "Working for the government."

"Now let's get down to what brings you to Francisco's? Is it the problem on the beach nearby?"

Antonio stopped talking when the waiter brought a silver serving set with cups and saucers, sugar and creamer, and a silver samovar containing hot coffee. Antonio said, "Allow me to pour."

Elaine said, "This is certainly the first time I've ever been treated like this when interviewing or questioning about a legal matter."

Antonio suggested, "Let's not play cat and mouse and get down to the facts. I know there must be a connection between the highway patrol findings on the beach and this restaurant or you wouldn't be here. Know I will help in any way I can. We have cameras and I personally keep an eye out for anything out of the ordinary in my establishment. I'm also the security for this restaurant, as well as having an interest in it. I retired and moved to the good ole United States and its relaxed way of life. I got bored, so went into business with Francisco's."

Elaine said, "I appreciate your candor. There was a body found on the beach a few hours ago. It hasn't been made known to the public yet. The body has not been formally identified the last time I heard. It was a woman. I believe she was a prominent businesswoman in this town and that's all I can say. The man, however that accompanied her to your restaurant, you might have noticed him. He was caucasian, around twenty-five or so with brown hair and was leaving the area driving a tan four door Chevrolet Malibu. The vehicle had an Arizona license plate. The couple ate lunch around noon."

Elaine continued as an afterthought: "Oh, I also found out from a previous interview that, to quote the person, 'He has a squeaky voice and was wearing cowboy boots.' If my profiling is correct, he would be nervous and possibly appear to be very uncomfortable in this situation. He would have followed the waiter and walked in front of the lady instead of allowing her to go first. Did you encounter someone similar or just like this man?"

"Yes, he came in and demanded a seat overlooking the ocean. I don't think this man knows he should tip to receive special seating!" Antonio said indignantly. Antonio added, "You seem to be right on the money. They were seated across the table from each other. He didn't allow her to speak, interrupting her continuously and ordering her food for her when she tried to order for herself. I seated them in an area where I could keep an eye on them. I thought he might be a guy that would run out on a woman and leave her holding the check. I have a tape of them and you will see what I mean."

Then Antonio said with a look of concern, "The guy reached in his pocket (and between you and me, that move could be trouble or not). He reached into his lower jacket pocket and not from the inside pocket which is where the majority of the men I know or have observed, including myself, keep small or valuable items."

Elaine was thinking of Antonio's observation. This was a sign of a man that did not think highly of women. This man had his intentions rebuffed too many times and he has to punish her or eliminate her from his life. Pete, as a psychopath, uses the gift of jewelry to help put these women off guard and persuade them to spend time with him.

Elaine's profiling so far is combined with what she already knows from the other killings and his M.O. Ms. Robertson rejected his advances many times before according to what her friend at work, Betty told us. Elaine thought to herself, *If Antonio has a recording of what transpired at the table, hopefully the expression on Ms. Robertson's face will be a good sign to confirm my profile of Pete.*

It would be normal for a person who was just given a gift, never mind an expensive one, to go along with that friend to finish a bottle of wine on the beach. It was then Elaine remembered there was no empty bottle found around the area of the murder. It would make sense that after killing Ms. Robertson, Pete would take the unfinished bottle of wine back to the car with him. Elaine made a note for TIA to keep an eye out for the wine bottle—should it be in his car when they find him.

Elaine asked for the full recording of what happened during their dining at Francisco's, as well as a copy of what they had for lunch complete with the name of the bottle of wine they purchased. Antonio volunteered to interview the waiter that served them when he came back for the dinner hours. Antonio said, "In fact, why don't you come back for dinner tonight."

Elaine said, "My sister is on vacation with me. Would a reservation for two be, okay?"

Antonio said, "Absolutely, no problem, bring her along."

Elaine said, "My sister doesn't know of my involvement with the murder and the local police as it is an ongoing investigation that even the public doesn't know about yet. As far as she is concerned, we are on our vacation for the Fourth of July celebrations on the beach."

"I'll give you the information surreptitiously that I find out from the waiter. The meal is on me tonight," Antonio said.

Elaine answered, "After I speak to my sister to see what time would be best for us, I'll call you. If you could work around that time and fit us in, that would be great!"
Antonio stood up, then pulled her chair out for her. He indicated to her their business interview was his pleasure. "I look forward to hearing from you and meeting your sister. Until tonight!" he spoke.

Elaine went to the lodge and called TIA. It took a few rings before Bill answered in his usual way: "Come on! Come on!"

Elaine laughed, "I'm calling to request a picture of the jewelry found on all the deceased women. Have you checked on who Pete is? Did the company he sells for give you his itinerary and did his stops coincide with the bodies found on the beaches? Also, with no evidence that would indicate who or why they were killed, I may have come up with the link between these women. See if they were in the vicinity of office supply companies. I may come up with a firm profile tomorrow. Check the overnight mail for a recording I'm sending, along with a written report of what information I have to date. I'll go to the coroner's office tomorrow. Cross your fingers we may have enough information to arrest this psychopath."

Elaine continued, "Have you gotten any information to send me about the missing student in Arizona? Please send it also. Our luck is holding as just a missing person, as none of the bodies look like her photo. Inquire, if possible, where the roommate of hers at the university went on her spring break. I really could use the cell phone number and name of the roomie. The case you gave me along with the missing student gave me little time to get much needed information. I would like to clear up both cases."

"Will do: over and out!" Bill said, and Elaine hung up.

Elaine called Lou and Lou was excited at the prospect of fine dining at the new restaurant on the beach.

Lou said softly, "So, what is this Antonio like? Is he good looking and why did he comp our dinner?"

Elaine said with a smile in her voice, "Tall, handsome and an ex-British copper...could have been mi-five or mi-six. He didn't say and I didn't ask. Look Sis, this is going to be a night of fun...for a change. I'll call Antonio and have him reserve a table for us at his convenience. I'll call you back."

Elaine was glad she was going to see Doc tomorrow at the morgue and get the final report on Ms. Robertson. She thought: *Doc will give me his interpretation of exactly what happened. As an expert, Doc will hopefully confirm my profile of Pete, or if I am still a long way off from nabbing this snake of a man.*

# Chapter 14

Elaine looked at Antonio's business card and dialed Francisco By The Beach restaurant. It rang, and someone picked up that sounded like Antonio; however, Elaine asked for him and said it was Elaine calling.

"Well Elaine, this is Antonio at your service! Are you and your sister going to join me for dinner this evening?"

Elaine answered, "Well, if the invitation is still open, yes! Would it be possible to meet after 6:30 p.m.?"

Antonio spoke softly, in a sexy tone of voice, "Shall we say around 7:00 p.m.? That's when I get off for the evening. It'll be my pleasure to have you two for my guests. There's live music and a small dance floor. We can mix good food with great company and I will help both of you pass the evening away."

Antonio continued, "I have the information you requested from the couple's waiter. Since your sister doesn't know of the murder as yet, I'll place my written information received from the server, their bill, and the disc recording their lunch inside your menu. I'll look forward to seeing you again and meeting your sister."

Elaine was even more interested in having dinner with Antonio then she thought she would be. By the way, he'd already planned the evening, business and pleasure all in one. She said pleasantly, "7:00 p.m. it is. We'll look forward to a fun evening," and before he could answer, she hung up.

Elaine called Lou and told her the time for their dinner engagement and what time she would pick her up.

Lou said, "I'm looking forward to having fun and good food, and may I say, if Antonio dances as well as he plans our evening, we may just have entered the end of the rainbow."

Elaine thought to herself, *If only this were true and the information needed to help catch this S.O.B. is in his notes along with the disc of his interview with the waiter. If they help in my profiling, I may well have found the pot of gold. Couldn't hurt if after Antonio meets Lou, he still saves a few dances for me, but then it is a business dinner... Darn.*

Elaine knew she couldn't try and out-dress Lou because no one could. Lou could fall in mud and come out smelling like a rose...as when she walks into any room, all eyes are on her. Not being left out in the cold when it comes to looks, Elaine was not jealous because being twins and not alike can be a good thing. An advantage in many ways, such as knowing what the other is going to do without asking and knowing there are advantages to being athletic, small, and intelligent. She thought, *Men don't expect you to sum them up into categories like I do when I profile. I must say, Antonio is very intriguing.*

Elaine looked into her magic bag to see what she had brought with her besides pants and boots. Ahh, there was one, one might call, "the little black dress." That would go well with the medium heeled black shoes she brought to go with her basic black suit needed for meetings. *Pull out my pearls, earrings and the ring that TIA gave her to wear when not scheduled for business but combining pleasure with business. If things go wrong, they will know immediately by the way, I twist it on my finger. One way for help and one way for them to keep track of her whereabouts.*

Lou called Elaine around 6:00 p.m. and informed her that she was ready anytime.

Elaine said, "In half an hour we can leave."

Lou said, "I'm glad I brought along something social to wear, if the moment arose."

Elaine thought to herself, *Sure you did, tell me something I don't know. I bet it'll be a lovely shade of green to go with her eyes and just a soft enough fabric to cling to her hourglass figure. Her shoes will not distract but attract her overall appearance. She will have a fabric stole draped over her shoulder in just a shade darker green than her dress, which she will casually use as a prop to bring attention to her sexy moves. Mind you, she doesn't do this on purpose, it is just...one might say...she was born with total poise and grace. That with her flowing hair...need I say more.*

Elaine picked up Lou and there wasn't anything she hadn't expected. Lou got into the car and glowed with expression when she said to Elaine, "Onward and upward, my dear sister!"

"As you wish my fair lady. All I can say is, behave yourself. Have fun but stay safe," Elaine said.

Lou asked, "Do you have your goodies on that will help TIA keep track of you should something make you feel uncomfortable?"

Elaine glanced at Lou, laughed and said, "I should have your luck with unwanted advances. Ha! Ha!"

They arrived at the parking lot and, as was the custom, parked the Rover close to the entrance so TIA could turn on the extra security system combining the surrounding area. This would include the whole entrance. Before they opened the door, a flash on the dash of the Rover appeared. A message: *"Check around the Rover before you get into it later. Each of you walk around the car and your bracelet will let you know if it's safe and there has been no one around your car and/or anything thrown under it. The all-clear sign is when you hear the doors unlock."*

Lou and Elaine began to laugh and said out loud, "One would think after all this time we would ever forget. What do they think, we are both in grade school? Oh, that's right, we were homeschooled."

Just then, a valet dressed in a cap and a shirt with the restaurant's logo approached their car. The valet asked, "Do you want valet parking?"

They let him know they were happy just where they were.

The valet piped up, "No problem, Antonio insisted I keep an eye out for you and see that you are taken care of. I'll escort you inside Francisco's!"

# Chapter 15

Lou looked at Elaine with a smile on her face and spoke softly, "I'm looking forward to meeting Antonio. He seems quite the gentleman."

The valet entered the restaurant and went up to the reservation desk and said, "These are Mr. Antonio's guests for the evening!" And he walked away.

The hostess escorted Elaine and Lou to Antonio's table, which was located in a private area far enough away from the music allowing them to talk without shouting. Also, they'd be able to dance without walking around lots of tables. She said, "Mr. Antonio will be with you shortly. Your waiter this evening will be William."

William was there to pull their chairs out and seat them. He said, "I'll return shortly, once I find out what Mr. Antonio suggests for your drinks."

Now picture this in this day and age: William is dressed all in black with a white shirt and black tie. He has a white towel draped over his forearm like something out of the movies. Elaine was the first to speak, "Lou, if the food is half as good as the atmosphere, we are in for a treat."

Lou then looked at Elaine and, in a whisper, said, "For dessert I think I will have that hunk coming our way."

Elaine casually half-turned her head in the direction Lou motioned to. Elaine laughed in a soft giggle said, "I saw him first. That is the infamous Mr. Antonio himself."

Lou said, "Yum! This is going to be fun."

Antonio strolled up with a smile on his face and stated, "I'm sorry to keep the two loveliest ladies in the restaurant waiting. It was closing time for me and I had to give the night shift a few instructions. I also took it upon myself to ask William to bring us a 2008 Nicolas Feuillatte Cuvee Palmes D'or Brut Millesime. I hope you will like it and if you don't, we can select something else."

William arrived with an assortment of appetizers to go with the champagne. Antonio told William, as he brought the menus for them, to wait awhile so they could enjoy some conversation while they sipped the champagne and enjoyed appetizers. William handed Mr. Antonio the menus.

Antonio gave Lou her menu first, then handed Elaine her menu containing the information Antonio had promised. Elaine brought her larger handbag so it would hold the disc and paper information. She smiled knowingly at Antonio and with a nod thanked him. His handling of the exchange of information almost confirmed Antonio as an ex-agent. Now, for her own curiosity, she would have to contact Bill and have him check further.

Antonio arranged for a man to dance with the lady that he wasn't dancing with. He would dance with one of the ladies until he saw Antonio take his partner back to the table and he would do the same. He then went back to another table.

Antonio suggested they order their meals and William would have their sommelier select the wine. Also, he thought soon the music would start up again and he hoped this would bring joy to them and maybe a bit of romance this evening. There was a note slipped to Antonio from the reservations desk and he had to excuse himself so he could look into a seating problem. Lou and Elaine smiled as he walked away.

"This is equal to some of the best restaurants in Europe," Elaine said to Lou, as she hadn't been to Europe for some time as she was kept busy in the USA. "I'm not complaining," Elaine said, "I just know this is the best restaurant I've been to in some time."

William came to the table and asked if he could remove their dishes. They indicated; he do so. A busboy came and removed the tray William had filled and went away quickly. William asked if they would enjoy some more champagne. They both nodded yes. "Your food will be served shortly after Mr. Antonio returns," William informed them.

Antonio returned and smiled at both of the ladies. "I took the liberty to order for you. If you don't like my selection let me know. It's the chef's special." Elaine and Lou seemed glad they didn't need to make a selection, as the menu was filled with so many delectable dishes it'd be very hard to choose.

Antonio mentioned he was proud to say there is no other restaurant as great as Francisco's in the area. Not even in Aberdeen. People drive from all over just for the service, atmosphere, dining, dancing, and privacy. I can attest that many a couple has become engaged in our place. A lot of businesses have been turned down on holidays when they wanted to hire the restaurant for their evening event. We have to request they select another time and day as we reserve the holidays mainly for our town and special patrons.

Antonio said to William who was just a few steps away, "We're ready to be served now along with the wine selected." He turned to the ladies and said with a smile, "Or would you ladies rather have coffee, tea, or me?" Antonio laughed at what he said, "My joke sounded better in my mind. I guess I have flown too much. It sounded funny when the stewardess said it. But then there were mostly men around me on the plane and not two exciting young women around me."

Lou was the first to laugh out loud and in her sexy voice, looking Antonio in the eye she said, "Not at all. I always wondered why the men didn't say that to the women on the plane. Instead, they just give us more drinks or nuts."

*Darn Lou, my twin always knows what to say in a situation like this. She knows how to put people at ease in touchy situations. Men can't resist her when she looks them in the eye and smiles. Well,* Elaine thought, *there goes my chance of dancing with an interesting, sexy man as the combo started to play a waltz.*

Antonio looked over at a table where another handsome gentleman sat with a drink in his hand. Antonio nodded his head and the gentleman came over to our table and asked Lou to dance. Antonio took Elaine's hand and said, "I believe this is our dance!" Antonio was a great dancer; however, Lou's new man danced like a professional and so did Lou. No wonder TIA sends her to be eye candy on dignitaries' arms in Europe and other places—that and she can speak almost every language she and her escort might encounter.

Antonio said to Elaine, "Lou's partner and I worked together in Europe. He retired shortly after me and decided to follow me to America. There isn't anything socially he can't do, as well as help me when I need more security on occasion. His name is Tom and I think Lou is probably the best dance partner he has had in some time. I have a feeling Tom should pay me for tonight's exquisite dance partner. I hope you don't mind settling for me?"

Elaine said, "You dance very well and I'm enjoying the evening, very much."

Antonio glanced at the table and William was bringing their food. Tom saw that Antonio and Elaine were headed for the table and he escorted Lou to her chair and pulled it out for her.

Antonio saw that Tom and Lou were having a good time and suggested to the ladies that Tom join them for dinner. Lou took about five seconds to answer, "That would be delightful!" William took care of the extra set-up. William showed Antonio the bottle of wine and poured some in Antonio's glass. He sipped it and motioned it was fine. William poured and put the rest of the bottle in the wine holder.

Tom and Lou were enjoying a private conversation and laughing. Antonio said to Elaine nodding toward Tom and Lou, "Hmm, I think we have a hit on our hands. That's what I call great luck as I have you all to myself—that's if you don't mind?"

Elaine blushed like a school girl and replied she was also glad not to have to dance with someone else.

The evening went by too fast as William had come and gone with the dishes and the combo had just finished their last set. Things were winding down in the restaurant, with most patrons already departing. Antonio took Elaine's hand and with a sigh in his voice said, "Unfortunately, it's time to call it a night. I must check tonight's receipts, cash out and schedule the staff for tomorrow's shifts."

Antonio stood up and asked, "Can I walk you to your car?" Tom by then was slipping Lou's stole over her shoulders and hand in hand they headed for the door.

Elaine and Lou had to walk around the sides of the Rover trying not to let on to the guys what they were doing so. Lou took Tom's hand and casually walked on her side of the Rover slow enough so the bracelet would have time to scan everything that might indicate the Rover had not been tampered with. Elaine did the same on her side with Antonio and all four of them ended at the back of the Rover. Elaine said how lovely the sunset and stars were this evening. They all agreed.

"I must get back to close things up," Antonio said while guiding Elaine back to her door, opening it. As she got in, Antonio bent down and gave her a soft, lingering kiss.

At the same time Lou and Tom were discussing something and then he opened the door for her and lightly kissed her and said, "Till tomorrow lovely lady!" And shut the door.

Antonio motioned to Elaine to roll down her window. He rested his elbows on the door and whispered to Elaine, "Honey, if this isn't a total one-of-a-kind Range Rover, I would say I am losing my touch. Looks to me like if you can't handle a situation, it will do it for you. Shades of the past!" He said so softly that she had to get closer to the window to hear what he was saying. As she got closer, he finished, kissed her lightly and said, "Come by tomorrow if you're free...any time."

Elaine rolled up the window and turned on the car. The dashboard blinked with a message: "*All was well.*" They both waved to the men as they slowly drove away.

Before Elaine could ask Lou about Tom, Lou started laughing and talking at the same time, "I think we had a few interesting moments this evening. At least I did!" Elaine acted as if it was just another day in her life. Lou said, "Tomorrow when you're working, I'm going to be escorted around this lovely small town. Then we will stroll on the beach ending with a picnic. Tom is off during the day and not working until the evening."

The fact there's a serial killer on the loose, Elaine isn't so sure about Lou going on a picnic. Not that she doesn't want Lou to enjoy herself with Tom, but she wants to make sure Lou is safe. Elaine tells her to wear all her goodies in case she needs help. Her day is going to be busy enough without having to worry about Lou until she wrapped things up at Doc's lab tomorrow. The coroner should have the information needed to prove beyond a reasonable doubt that Pete is the killer, along with the combined information from Bill and TIA.

# Chapter 16

When they got to the lodge, Elaine pulled up in front of Lou's place and let her out. She waited until Lou was inside. A message came on the dashboard: *"I'm in and all is well. Get some sleep and call me in the morning and we can have breakfast together before you go to work."*

Lou waited until she thought Elaine would be inside her room and called her on her cell. Elaine answered and said, "What can I do for you Lou?"

Lou replied, "I plan on having a great day tomorrow with Tom. I wanted you to know I'll be sure to have all my goodies on and hope you do the same. If you need me, I will ditch Tom and fly in low altitude so I can save the day." Lou laughed and joked some more then seriously said, "Elaine, do not take any chances in whatever you will be doing. Put the Rover transmitter on so wherever you are I will get a message of how to find you and the best route to take. I will be notifying TIA I'm going to your rescue. I'm going to sleep after my shower, you do the same, Sis!" And she hung up.

Elaine thought, *Boy, if Lou only knew why I wanted her to stay alert.* With the way the evening went and both guys coming on to them, she just wanted Lou to be as careful as she would be until she had Bill do a search on Antonio and Tom.

Elaine checked in with Bill and he said, "Come on! Come on! There goes our ESP again. I was going to call you to let you know you are to call the lodge office and ask for Mary Jo. She has a package for you with the information you requested. Still don't have itinerary on Pete and we haven't located his car."

Elaine said, "I have something you should check on immediately. I might have run into a situation here. I met a man named Antonio and don't have his last name. I interviewed him at his restaurant, Francisco's By The Beach, where the couple went to eat before they found the body on the beach. I gave Antonio Elaine's business card. He looked surprised that I was a criminal profiler and called over someone to take his desk while we sat at a table where we could talk in private."

First thing out of his mouth was, "I think you have the wrong place and I can't understand why you would need to talk in private to me?" He then said it must have something to do with the incident on the beach, "Am I correct?"

Elaine told him that a deceased person was found on the beach and there is reason to believe she had lunch there earlier and needed Antonio's help verifying some facts. "He volunteered some personal information about himself," she said, "saying he came from Europe to America to retire and becoming bored in retirement, bought into the restaurant. The position he held was working in the back roads of Europe investigating certain things for the government. He seemed interested in the intrigue and happy to help."

Elaine continued, "What I need you to do, Bill, is to do a background check and also one for an acquaintance of his named Tom—no last name as yet. He too retired from the government in Europe and came to the USA. He helps with security when Antonio needs him.

"Antonio is running the restaurant and 'security.' He invited us to join him for dinner. During the course of the evening, both Antonio and Tom came on to us strongly and I need to eliminate them as possible suspects in the murder. Antonio seems like an open book, but who knows? Bill, do your magic and let me know what you find out, sooner than later. He came off in my mind as being with MI-5 of MI-6.

"Lou is going to see the town with Tom in the morning so you can understand my urgency. She isn't aware that my case may involve this man or both men. Let me say I hope not, as they are very nice gentlemen. But then, most predators act like the nice guy next door. An ounce of prevention in this case. I want to know Lou will be okay.

"Now that I know you haven't found anything further about Pete, I can't rule out anyone. Doc will hopefully have all I need to finish this profile. Now I assume you have included in the package photos of the jewelry found on the other dead women along with the whereabouts of the roomie of the student that is missing from Arizona. At least her phone number. I hope you have been able to find out if her parents were expecting her to go home for spring break.

"I hope to close part of Pete's profile today and with his itinerary from his company, try to figure out where he might find his next victim. If he has the missing student and in his state of mind, he could very well have his next victim. Time is of the essence. I hope to hear from you tomorrow morning Bill. You may just save another woman's life."

Bill said, "I'll get on it right away and make it a high priority with TIA staff. I'll contact you by phone and also send the information package, ASAP. Over and out Elaine." As Bill hung up, she went to shower and hopefully get a good night's sleep. She thought to herself, *I hope Antonio and Tom are who they say they are!* "From my mouth to god's ears!" She spoke out loud.

Elaine reread the paperwork on all the women that were found killed, trying to ascertain if there was anything besides the jewelry that was similar with each victim. It certainly wasn't their looks as they were all very different looking. However, all were working for an office supply company. Their autopsies showed they had recently consumed food and alcohol. This indicated he would take them to lunch, give them a gift, and then continue the lunch date walking on the beach gaining their trust. As a salesman, he probably didn't make that much money so he most likely would take the women to cheaper cafes/restaurants.

Ms. Robertson's friend Betty said Pete had asked her out many times. Ms. Robertson had a very strong demeanor and would always abruptly reject his offer, dismissing him with a sneer. Being rebuffed so many times would have made the man/psychopath really angry. During his next visit he prepared himself to give her a gift, but also knew he had to up his ante and pick out a venue she would be impressed with and not refuse. The only thing he could think of was Francisco's By The Beach. Enter the psychopath's personality and all the reasoning disappeared. He had to get her to go with him regardless; his desire was burning deep in is soul.

Elaine hopes the information she receives from Bill and Doc will confirm her suspicions. Ms. Robertson was so much like his controlling, displeasing mother that he has and must get her to go with him. He knew that if she didn't oblige him, he would just kill the first unsuspecting woman he might encounter. The urge for revenge was too great. If this Pete isn't the killer, then let's hope it isn't Tom, and Lou is safe.

Elaine made her way to Doc's lab looking forward to what facts may have come to light. Doc was in the lab with a smile on his face indicating he had some good news to share.

Doc mentioned to Elaine that she should prepare herself for what she was about to see. "It's okay Doc, this isn't my first encounter with something out of the ordinary," Elaine said with anticipation for what he was about to show her.

Doc proceeded to uncover the top part of the body to explain quickly and succinctly what his findings held: "If you look at the bruising on her neck, this coincides with an attempted choke hold wherein using the forearm and with his free hand grip the wrist, pulling it back, collapsing the airway causing a transient cerebral ischemia. This hold results in weakness on both sides of the body, difficulty speaking, slurred speech, dizziness, vertigo, double vision, loss of coordination, and finally loss of consciousness resulting from a lack of oxygen. This hold didn't fracture the larynx or hyoid bone. She must have appeared dead so he released the choke hold. She then could have regained consciousness within thirty seconds and at that time tried to fight him, scratching him either on his neck, face or arm. I was able to find DNA traces and other particles from under her fingernails. He must have been so angry she dared to fight him; he threw her limp but not dead body down on the rocky sand with such brute force, this caused the coup de grace."

Elaine watched as he gently turned her over to show Elaine the cuts and bruises visible on the back of her head and torso.

"This time, there was absolutely no question that she had succumbed to this new assault on her person. I must say, it was as though he lost all control of his senses. There was no way he was going to let her survive," Doc said.

Even though Elaine had similar experiences in other cases, this one seemed to overwhelm her with grief. Elaine thanked Doc for his fast, practical, and knowledgeable explanation, stating that with what she had already learned and his information, it should give them the missing connection in this case.

# Chapter 17

Elaine went out to the parking lot and did her usual exterior checking of the Rover and as the doors automatically unlocked, she got in and waited a few seconds to decide what her next move might be. She hadn't heard from Lou, so she pushed the stone on her bracelet and waited to see if the stone turned black, indicating Lou was unsure of her circumstances or in trouble. This didn't happen and Elaine's stone went back to normal. *Thank god,* she thought, and decided to go to Francisco's By The Beach for coffee and a mid-morning sweet treat.

She drove up to the front entrance of the restaurant, secured the Rover, and TIA took over the car. Elaine walked into the restaurant and Antonio was there at the registration desk. He had a smile on his face and motioned to the girl that was folding napkins to take over and told her to bring over coffee and a sweet tray for two at his table.

Antonio motioned for Elaine to follow him to his private table that allowed him to see the entry and front desk. With delight he said, "I am so glad you are able to join me this morning. I was ready for a break and it certainly is much better to have coffee with a beautiful woman and not alone." Antonio smiled and added, "I hope your meetings this morning proved helpful?"

Elaine quipped, "I won't be able to tell until I combine all the information collected. Once this is done, I'll have a complete profile of the perp."

Antonio shook his head and reminisced, "Well, you looked encouraged with the news and that's great. I can certainly say I don't miss that part of my past, the waiting and anticipation of learning the facts."

"Just what was your past job and what company did you work for? I know you said you worked for the government but that was all!" Elaine piped up taking advantage of this turn in the conversation.

Antonio got a smile on his face (it was a smile like he had on last evening when he was about to tell a joke). He said trying to talk like an actor in the movies, "If I tell you, I will have to kill you".

Elaine thought, *Well, I guess that means none of your business.* Seems I will have to wait till I get back to the lodge to know what Bill found out about Antonio and Tom.

Elaine checked on Lou once more, pressing the stone on her bracelet. The stone showed no abnormalities. Elaine knew Lou was okay, so far.

Antonio asked, "Would you and Lou enjoy dinner here again tonight?

Elaine said, "I'm sorry, but I have other plans for this evening. We'll just sample the lodges food as I am expecting phone calls. Hopefully, supplying much needed information for my case. I guess you know all about working for the government and waiting for information? I assume it was for either MI-5 or MI-6?"

Antonio said, "Why do you think that?"

Elaine smiled coyly and said, "Just because of your comments. Tell me if I am wrong?" Elaine thought she might just have hit a nerve by the way he asked how I arrived at my assumptions. This time Elaine just smiled and sipped her coffee.

"Well," Elaine said, "an hour has passed and I'm afraid I have one more meeting before I go back to the lodge."

Antonio pulled her chair out and asked if he could walk her to the car.

Elaine touched another stone on her bracelet sending TIA an instant message stating she would check the car and unlock the door herself.

Antonio opened the car door and said, "If you have a break this evening, please come back as I'll be here."

Elaine drove to the lodge and stopped in front of Lou's room, knocked on the door. *Hmmm, she hasn't returned from her day with Tom and she told me he was working tonight. It seems she should be back by now.* Elaine went to her room and there was a package inside the door. She hoped it was the information on Antonio and Tom that she had requested from Bill and the other answers needed to rule out anyone other than Pete as the killer.

Elaine was starting to worry about Lou. Elaine was about to call TIA/Bill and see if he has found out about Antonio and Tom's identity and their history.

Elaine called Bill and said in a gush of words, "I need you to contact Lou's handler and have him put a trace on her location immediately!"

Bill said, "Slow down Elaine...why are you worried about Lou? Before you start explaining and to ease your concern, I have the trace in progress and they'll make contact with Lou within moments." Then Bill said, "What makes you think Lou might be in trouble?"

Elaine said, "Since I haven't received any definitive information from you or TIA about Pete, namely, his last name, trip itinerary and the fact no one has received material from his employer, I have to assume he might not be the killer and the killer may still be in the area. With all the facts I gave you and TIA...in my mind I feel I should have something concrete to profile. Knowing his first name, make and color of car and the fact the car is registered in Arizona, I should have more facts from your end. Only this combined information will assure me I am on the right track."

Elaine continued with a deep breath, "The guys Lou and I met last evening became more complex when Lou accepted an invitation to be shown around town with an ending of their day with a picnic on the beach. I couldn't tell Lou not to go and blow my case investigation. That, with the fact she wouldn't have believed this of Tom and that he could be a possible danger. Combine all of this and a picnic on the beach, well you're damn right I'm concerned! She still has not returned."

Bill said, "Now I understand—especially when it involves the beach and a very beautiful woman, even if she is a trained agent. Because these two fellows are from Europe the agents are having to check every connection they have. Why don't you call the restaurant and ask Antonio if he has heard from Tom as Lou was with him for the day and you are concerned you haven't heard from her. Ask him if he would mind calling him to check his ETA for work tonight."

Elaine said, "Sounds good Bill, but keep pushing on where and what these two guys did in Europe."

Bill said, "Don't worry, I was just given a heads-up from the powers that be that they were closing in on answers for both Pete and the two fellows you and Lou have gotten involved with."

Elaine said softly and rather abruptly, "What are my earned vacations for if not some romance somewhere. I did do you a favor when I accepted one case that has now turned into two."

Bill said, "Now, now my sweet young lady, there is room for romance but not for both of you at the same time...later, ten-four, over and out!"

Elaine was anxious so she got up, brushed her teeth, took a shower and dressed casually. She checked her phone: no messages. She called Lou's room and with one ring Lou answered.

Lou said, "Sis you must have ESP. I just got in and I have lots to tell you."

Elaine said for her to come over to her room and have a drink so they could talk.

Lou said for her to give her a few minutes to freshen up.

"Take your time, I'm just glad you're okay!" Elaine said.

# Chapter 18

As Elaine hung-up, she received a call from Bill. Bill said, "You can stop worrying! Lou is fine and evidently, she has had a fun-filled day. Two things you might be glad to know. One is that the parents of the missing student were not expecting her home for spring break. Here is the name of her roomie...it's Carol. She is going to Washington with her parents in their RV for the Fourth of July celebrations. They figure this will probably be the last trip for all of them to be together as a family because their daughter is no longer a child, but a grown woman. By the way, Carol's cell phone number is included in the package you will be receiving. I wouldn't call her until after we obtain the information on Pete. You should work on one case at a time. I agree with you that we want to get this S.O.B. before he has time to kill another woman. I want us to stay on track with this case. Hold on my lady, the agents have some information for me and I have to take it...we will talk as soon as I find out more," and before she could answer, Bill hung-up.

This phone call from Bill made Elaine's' day and the fact that Lou was safe and sound in her room.

There was a light knock on the door and in a whisper Lou said, "It's little ole me."

"Come on in!" Elaine said as Lou entered the room in her usual sexy stroll. Elaine thought to herself, *Darn, there she goes again, an entrance as if there was royalty on the other side of the door, unfortunately it's only her tomboy sister.*

"Well, Lou, you have some explaining to do. No heads-up from you all day. I didn't know for sure if you were okay."

Lou quipped, "Oh, so that's why I was called and asked what I'm doing and where I was at."

Elaine said, "You're damn right! There are things going on in this little ole town that you were not aware of!"

Lou stated, "Not to worry Sis, as I was in good hands as I was out with Tom. Remember the ESP we have works well and I told you I was going to see the town with him and end with a picnic on the beach. Tom said he had a change of plans for today because of what Antonio told him. There had been a killing on the beach and Tom said we would stay away from there for my safety. He took me to his rancho/winery...way up in the hills at the edge of town." Lou got comfortable and began her tale of the day's events with great animation. Lou said, "This is how the day went word for word after Tom drove me to his rancho/winery."

Lou took a deep breath and began. "Upon arrival Tom said, 'I met a lovely family that previously owned this property. They fell on hard times and I had just retired so I purchased the rancho/winery, along with more acreage that abutted the winery. I fell in love with the family and made a contract with them to live there and run the business, awarding them a percent of all profits. Plus, their children were going off to college.' (Tom suspected that is why they needed the money. Putting two children through college is a very expensive undertaking). 'That made me think purchasing the land next to the rancho/winery would be a good idea. Mama Maria and her husband's children were hoping to take over from their parents when they could no longer do the work. I suggested part of the new land should be cultivated and more grape trees/vines be planted. Hopefully, starting to produce wine by the time they graduated in three years. I would also like to add a few out-buildings on the additional land for some of my toys. Besides the large rancho house, there are already many buildings on the property including a small quaint casa.'

"Tom continued, 'This casa is where I live. Mama Maria keeps it spotless for me. It really is all the space I need at this point in my life. We agreed that Mama Maria's family would live in the large rancho until the children took over. At that time they would move into my small casa and I would live in the large rancho.' Tom mentioned, 'We didn't transfer the title yet so the children could use that address for a discount on their tuition which they would be receiving living in that specific area.' Just then Mama Maria came out and hugged Tom and also gave me a hug and a light motherly kiss on my forehead. Tom smiled at me, as I must have blushed. Mama Maria told Tom to show me the rancho and upon his return, that she'd have some more palatable food than what was packed in his picnic basket earlier this morning. Tom told her, as he gave her a son-like kiss, she always made the sunshine brighter. It was Mama Maria's turn to blush. We walked the property and Tom said, 'I'm just learning about running a winery and really not able to tell you much about the different types of grapes yet. The moment I first saw this rancho/winery from the road, I just fell in love with it. That along with the fact I would have a ready-made family to run it, I knew I'd struck gold.'

"We walked back to a large covered patio with a long table able to seat about twenty people. There in an area a little further away was a table set for two with a large vase of wildflowers set on a beautiful white lace tablecloth. It was overlooking a beautiful valley with the hills shadowed in the background. Flowers, and all the best of everything was arranged just for us.

Mama Maria walked over to us and said, 'I will bring you good food to eat, not that restaurant food.' Tom said laughingly, 'Now, Mama.' She smiled and said, 'I know you work at a fancy restaurant but nothing beats fresh organic food.' Tom said to me with a wink in his eye, 'Being that this is an organic rancho it certainly helped sweeten the deal.' We ate and drank and talked for what seemed like hours. Tom said softly, 'Honey, if you want to see the rest of the good ole town, we had better cut this luncheon short.'

"Tom pulled Lou's chair out and took her hand in his and started to walk up a different path from which they had arrived. I stopped and looked questioningly at Tom and said, 'This isn't the way to the car.' Tom laughed and said, 'But this is the way I want to take you!'" Lou finished, but her story wasn't quite complete. You see, Lou was an agent first and a woman second. Her instinct as an agent took over and she tapped on her transmitter to record their conversation from this point on:

Lou said,"Where are we going, haven't we seen all the property at the winery?"

Tom said, "Lou my dear, you are in for a treat as we will see the town better and faster in my helicopter."

Tom started his pre-flight inspection and motioned for Lou to come aboard. Pretending she didn't know much about flying she ask him what kind of a helicopter it was. "This is my private Eurocopter 120 Colibri. It's a six-seater, single engine, light utility helicopter and is about as green as you can get. Designed aiming to reduce pollutant emissions, low noise signatures and increase fuel efficiency in accordance with the Green Rotorcraft

European Clean Sky Joint Technology Initiative." Lou mentioned she liked the red letters, numbers, and symbols displayed on the tail, which she repeated loud enough to record over the whirring of the helicopter blades.

Tom yelled, "Come on girl, you are in for a treat." They flew along the beach and being a small town there wasn't much to look at except the small boats with people fishing on them. "Look at where the boat's land on the beach," Tom said over his headset. "That is where the town's people purchase the fresh catch of the day. Look close and you can see a few boats have already filled their quota for the day and are hopefully selling all of their catch."

Tom said to Lou, "Shall we land on the helicopter pad at the restaurant as we go by where the poor woman's body was found? I'll take you to your lodge using Antonio's company car. It is used for taking home people unable to drive safely. Cabs are far and few between in this town."

Lou responded, "Sounds like a good plan to me."

They landed without incident and once everything was shut down, Tom went in to fetch the keys and retrieve the car from the back of the restaurant. Shortly, Tom pulled up in front in a Mercedes. Lou thought to herself, "I would say this beats a cab for transportation any day."

Tom pulled into the lodge and since they never give out our room number to anyone. Lou asked to be dropped off at the office to check messages. The office staff had been instructed not to divulge any information concerning any guests staying on the premises. The office help knew that not abiding by this rule meant being fired on the spot and probably being struck by lightning. No excuses were tolerated, even if the office help knew the person asking.

Lou said she went into the office and watched to see Tom was out of sight and then walked to her room. She then received Elaine's call.

"And that's how it happened," said Lou.

Elaine nodded her head and said, "Well Lou, you sure had an exciting day!"

Lou laughed and said, "Indeed I did. I have to say I was sneaky and recorded some of our conversation as we were taught, 'agent first.'"

Elaine broke in and they both said in unison: "Woman last."

They sipped on their drinks and Lou asked, "What time are we going to eat?"

Elaine frowned and answered, "Well, Antonio asked if we wanted to come over and eat at Francisco's, but we should expect them both to be working. So, I said no...but I could have you call and ask if they could take a short break and such, if we did end up there for dinner."

Lou said, "I just might do that and get a reservation." Lou made the call and told Elaine their reservation was set for 7:00 p.m. "Does that suit you Elaine?"

Elaine replied, "Yes, however let's dress casually as I don't want to wear the same little black dress. I think I will have to plan ahead next time we go on vacation."

"Gee! Elaine, "You will have to just do what I do and buy clothes as needed during the trip. Write it off as a company expense."
Elaine shrugged saying, "I usually wear daytime clothes and rarely go out in the evening. TIA keeps me very busy. Lou, I think I might have to ask TIA to extend me some better cases that would require some time for socializing."

Lou excused herself and said she wanted to rest, shower and then be ready around 6:30 p.m. "See you then, Sis!"

As Lou left, Elaine grabbed the heap of papers sitting on the table and leafed through them. There was absolutely nothing new or of interest in the package. Elaine thought to herself, "Darn this was a stressful day, with all the worry about Lou and my having to light a fire under Bill to get better information. I know I had my shower earlier, but I think I'll go soak in the tub and take a bubble bath, turn on some soft music and sip a glass of wine. Hmm, that will beat a nap anytime!"

Elaine got out of the tub and did all the things a woman does when getting ready to go out. *Casual dress for me is a lovely silk blouse, a jacket that is both comfortable and color coordinated along with designer jeans that fit like a glove and cowboy style short boots*, she thought. She looked in the mirror and said to herself, "Looking good girl."

Elaine looked at her watch and it was almost time for her to pick up Lou. Elaine checked for messages to see if anything further was received while she was soaking in the tub. No such luck. *Well, what the heck*, she thought, *I will just forget about work tonight and join in the fun while Antonio works the front desk unless he has something else in mind.*

Lou was at the front door waiting for Elaine. That was a change for Lou to be waiting for me instead of the opposite. Lou liked to always be where she could make a grand entrance. *I guess Lou is saving that entrance for Tom to see. She must really have had a good time with him. Hmm, that's a first!* she thought.

Lou, dressed in a light teal sweater, dark brown slacks in the latest style from a European designer and soft kid leather Italian boots, got gracefully into the Rover. Elaine thought to herself, *Wow, my Sis looks fabulous as always.* Lou smiled at Elaine as she knew what Elaine was thinking. Sometimes it is fun to be a twin, as you can communicate without saying a word.

"Now I hope we get a spot just outside the front entrance to the restaurant," Lou said.

Elaine smirked and added, "I don't think we will have a problem parking as I am sure Antonio or Tom will have it reserved for two of the best, most wonderful women who have entered their lives since they retired." Lou and Elaine laughed at that assumption.

As predicted, a spot was waiting for them, along with the valet, to open the car doors. He opened Lou's door first and then ran around to the driver's door and gallantly handed Elaine out of the driver's side. With both of them holding onto each of his arms, he led them up the steps to the front door. He ushered them in and smiling said with much fanfare, "Welcome ladies to Francisco's By The Beach!"

Antonio was waiting and Tom was standing behind the reservation desk. They both chuckled at the valet and Antonio said, "Ahh, lovely ladies! It's so nice to see you and to enjoy your lovely company again tonight," as he took Elaine's hand.

Lou was checking out Tom and he was eyeing her as well. Tom smiled and said to Lou, "I know we just saw each other a while ago, but I've missed you." Lou smiled back and said, "I missed you too, it was such a lovely day!"

Antonio took them to a private table away from the crowd (so to speak) and ask the ladies to order whatever they desired. "Drinks first and then I will bring over tonight's menu," as he winked at Elaine. *Oh, I think he has another message for me. I hope so*, she thought. Antonio excused himself and went to the front desk to say hello to a party of four that just entered the restaurant.

It was just a few moments when William was at their table to find out what they wanted to drink. Lou said, "I think I will try one of your signature before dinner drinks. Could I see the drinks menu please?"

Elaine looked at William but before she could say what she wanted, he suggested he bring a sample selection of the days beverage specials for them to try. "What the heck?" Elaine said looking at her Sis, then they both said in unison, "Sounds great!"

Antonio was busy at the reservations desk as Tom came over to give Lou a kiss on her forehead and welcomed her. He then looked at Elaine and said, "I'm very happy to see both of you this evening. Unfortunately, I must get back to the front. I will see you both later when time permits after the rush hour."

# Chapter 19

William came over with a selection of three kinds of pre-dinner cocktails for each of them. William explained each beverage to them. "First, we have a Canadian Polar Bear (equal parts, crème de cacao and crème de menthe shaken not stirred over ice. This concoction tastes like an After Eight Mint or Peppermint Paddy). Next we have the Australian Cucumber Collins (dry gin, elderflower cordial, lemon juice, thin cucumber slices topped off with soda water and ice. This drink is stirred, not shaken). Last, but not least, we have the Italian Negroni (gin, red semi-sweet vermouth and Campari, garnished with orange peel poured over ice). Enjoy ladies and should you want more let me know." He walked back toward the kitchen as Antonio was on his way with menus.

Lou and Tom were smiling and ogling each other at a distance. Antonio gave Lou a menu first and then handed Elaine hers. He pressed his hand on hers and spoke, "Check the back of the menu; you have seen everything inside." Antonio saw Lou was still watching Tom so he said to Elaine, "I think I may have just helped you find out what is necessary to end your search for Pete, at least put you where you want to be."

She smiled and said softly to him, "Thanks Antonio, please come back."

There was a disc and a note under the menu. She put the note inside her menu to read it so Lou wouldn't know. The note read:

> *The information on Pete you wanted is copied on the disc. I went out to fix a camera in the parking lot I thought was broken. It wasn't broken, and all this time it was working but there was dust or something that made it blurry on the screen. The video is clear now as with all the high winds and rain showers we have been having, the dust must have been washed away. To my surprise, the man that was with Ms. Robertson for lunch came out clearly, as well as his car and Arizona license plate, big as life. You can also see he has a bottle of wine with him. Pete then motioned the beach and escorted her to the area you described as the murder scene. I hope this helps and that it will free you up to enjoy some time with me should you wish to. I certainly would like that!*

Elaine caught Antonio's eye and nodded along with a great big smile. Antonio then turned and went back to accommodating his patrons.

Elaine and Lou were both not as hungry as they thought after the sampler of pre-dinner drinks. William came to the table and asked if they would like more drinks. They decided they should eat. Elaine spoke first and requested a Caesar salad with grilled chicken and she started to say garlic bread but corrected herself and requested their homemade biscuits and added, "Yum!"

Lou said, "I think I will have the same."

William asked, "What they would like to drink with their dinner?"

This time Lou spoke first and said, "Perrier please!"

And Elaine said, "Make that two."

Lou asked Elaine, "What was Antonio whispering to you? Was he speaking sweet nothings in your ear?"

Elaine looked at Lou and said to her in exasperation, "Whatever do you mean? He just hoped I had a good day. As you know Lou, I have been busy on a case. Fun and games will have to come later. I will say though, I do find him most interesting."

Lou laughed and said, "When you play that 'who cares attitude' with me, I know you are more than interested. Too bad I have to get to Copalis Beach so fast Sis, I am sure we both would enjoy spending more time here with those two hunks!"

"I really didn't know this road trip you have going with the company was something out of the ordinary. You know what I mean?" Elaine said in a soft voice, "I can truly say this personal encounter with Antonio is a first for me."

The salads were being served with hot biscuits and a tall bottle of Perrier for each.

Lou and Elaine had a lot to be thankful for and bowed their heads and softly said a blessing before starting to eat. They glanced at each other and held up their glass of Perrier to toast to "the good life."

Just then both Antonio and Tom came walking up to the table and sat down by the ladies. "Well, what have we here, teetotalers in our midst?" Antonio said to Tom.

Tom laughingly said, "Maybe they need a dance or two in between bites as they are eating cold food tonight." The combo was set up and started to play a slow romantic dance. Tom extended his hand to Lou and off they went to the dance floor where they started dancing like professionals.

Antonio looked at Elaine and said, "I'm not the best dancer, but I hope you like just dancing close, enjoying the person you are with."

"I certainly am," Elaine murmured with a smile on her face as she snuggled close in his arms and added, "I like you just the way you are."

Antonio came back with, "Now honey, you aren't just saying that because I gave you what I think is the information needed to round up your case?"

Elaine laughed and replied, "Well now Mr. Antonio, there is a saying that is for both men and women and that is 'never kiss and tell.'" With that, Antonio gave her a light romantic kiss on the top of her head. *Darn*, Elaine thought, *this is the first time I'm sorry I'm not a little taller*. The dance was over and Antonio motioned to Tom that they had better go help at the front desk.

The ladies finished their dinner and walked towards Antonio and Tom who were waiting to escort them to their Rover. Antonio said, "Rose will watch the desk while we see that you two are safely ensconced in the car." Antonio took Elaine's hand and gave it a soft squeeze. "I am so glad you changed your mind and came by this evening. How about you gals come over here around 9:00 a.m. Tom said he would like to take us to his rancho for one of Mama Marias' great breakfasts. That way, we can talk a little longer before you ladies head on your way. Tom will mention it to Lou."

Elaine said, "That sounds lovely. We will make sure we arrived in time for the helicopter ride to the rancho. Antonio, would it be possible to have another one of your business cards for my records?"

Antonio laughingly said, "You mean so you can add me to your little black book?"

Once they were at the car, they followed their usual routine around the car. Everything was safe and the doors automatically unlocked. Tom asked Lou, "Would you like to have breakfast at the rancho tomorrow? Elaine knows about the invite and she thought it would be wonderful, especially after hearing so much about the property."

Lou said, "Only if you give me your business card."

Tom said, "Well honey, I will do better than that, I will make sure my highly confidential personal cell phone number is on it. Make sure to put that number in your little black book under 'important.'" As he opened the door for her and before letting her get in, he pulled her close and gave her a long lingering kiss.

On the other side of the Rover, Antonio was doing the same. He leaned down and said, "I'll see you ladies tomorrow at 9:00 am." He winked and shut the door. Lou and Elaine looked at each other smiling.

Lou said, "Elaine, I know we both asked TIA to do a background check on Antonio and Tom. Today, just before we got in the helicopter, I went into agent mode and copied down the make and tail number. I will text you the information for your files in case you every need it."

Elaine said, "About tomorrow, I have to call in some new information that came to light, which I hope might conclude the case I'm working on. If all goes well, I will be able to make it for breakfast." Elaine dropped Lou off at her room and waited until she was inside and safe, then she proceeded to her own room, as if Lou needed her help Elaine laughed to herself.

Elaine could not wait to call Bill and give him the newly received information. She would have the note and disc from Antonio dispatched to him posthaste. The disc showed Pete in the area with Ms. Robertson, his car license, and the bottle of wine he must have taken with him after he killed her. The bottle should still be in his car if he hasn't discarded it somewhere.

Elaine phoned Bill and said, "My profile is complete and as far as I'm concerned, that psychopath did kill her. The evidence on the disc is a slam dunk. 'Case closed' and ready to turn over to the local highway patrol."

Bill said to Elaine, "I received the itinerary of Pete's next stop and with the highway patrol working at their end; they should have him in custody and no one will ever know we had anything to do with it. That was damn good work Elaine!"

Bill continued, "Now look young lady, when you get to the cottage you can start your vacation after you contact Carol and find out what her roomie did for spring break. I pray she knows and we can assure her parents she is okay. Drive safe and let us know when you are heading for Copalis Beach and the cottage."

Bill said, "One other thing. I think you should travel in fast mode as we need Lou to do her thing at Ocean Shores. When we know you are on your way, we will clear the road with the help of the highway patrol."

"Will do Bill, we have plans for breakfast and will get on the road soon after that. I will notify you so you can handle all the details involved in Rover's fast mode," Elaine replied.

# Chapter 20

Elaine and Lou grabbed a quick coffee the next morning and decided they should dress for driving as they must leave right after breakfast. "I look forward to seeing Mama Maria again. She is a fabulous cook and she has a very nice family. She cares for Tom and spoils him terribly. One can easily see that the feelings are mutual." Lou smiled.

Elaine and Lou checked out of the hotel and headed towards Francisco's. On the way, Elaine told Lou that they were to put the peddle to the metal or fast mode per TIA instructions on their way to the cottage.

"You are going to be surprised at Tom's rancho. Too bad we don't have more time so I could possibly check out even more surprises he has hidden away. If everything else is as good as his taste in property—well, you get my drift," laughed Lou.

As they pulled into Francisco's parking lot, Antonio directed them to park in the back. They parked and then were ushered into the passenger seats of the helicopter. Tom flew and Antonio was for lack of another word was the co-pilot. "I don't even know if Antonio can fly! That in itself tells me I need to have more time to find out more about Antonio," Elaine said.

"Now who is finding their new guy interesting. Sis, you've got to get out more; that is all I can say," Lou said with a smile on her face as Elaine poked her. Lou chuckled and said, "Don't worry, they can't hear us with the noise from the helicopter. They are probably wondering about us, too."

Antonio turned and looked at them a short time later and said, "Here we are! We will land near the hanger and then walk down to the patio where Tom says Mama Maria is waiting for us."

Tom said, "I hope you enjoy her cooking. She learned from her mama, grandmother, etc. A multi-generation of cooks in her family passed down their recipes; however, I think she added her own style to most of them. Best food ever!" Tom gushed.

Antonio looked at Tom and told him, "Now don't you get any silly ideas about starting up a restaurant next to me. You are needed at Francisco's!"

Tom said to Antonio, "Like that could ever happened. My private time is thin enough without taking on another huge project." He winked and they both laughed.

Just as they arrived at the covered patio, Mama Maria came out of the kitchen and was introduced to Elaine. Smiling Mama Maria announced, "Breakfast is ready. I made for you this morning a smorgasbord of 'all you can eat breakfast.' A serve yourself table full." Mama laughed as she looked lovingly at the expression on Tom's happy face.

Tom ushered everyone over to the table and said, "Ladies first."

Lou whispered to Elaine, "Oh look how lovely everything looks. Flowers on the table, perfect place settings, a small side table with orange juice, water and everything for coffee and tea. We might think we are at home. Maybe we should invite them to visit us when we return to Malibu, California. Just to show them, we also know how to live well."

Elaine suggested, "If my hunch is right about their previous life in Europe, they probably already know all about us."

Once they were seated with their plates filled with a little of everything, they held hands and said a short blessing. This was not expected of the men, but the ladies were happy to know they all seemed to be brought up the same.

They were all eating, talking, and laughing when Mama Maria came by and asked how everything was. "Perfect Mama Maria, I believe I tried everything," Elaine said with a smile on her face patting her tummy.

"I can attest to that," Lou said.

Antonio piped up, "Mama, I can say without a doubt you surely outdid yourself. Are you sure you won't come and cook for me or at least give me your recipes?"

Tom laughed and told Antonio, "Look here buddy, you can't have her. I saw her first. Besides, she's family."

Lou spoke softly to Mama Maria, "I wanted you to know that I have traveled most of the world and not many people cook like you. Keep your recipes secret and just pass them down from generation to generation."

Mama Maria smiled and moved behind Tom's chair with her arms draped around him she said with tears in her eyes, "Your kind friends are welcome here always!"

Looking at his watch Tom suggested they head back to Francisco's. "You ladies' have a long drive ahead."

"Wait!" said Mama Maria. "Tom told me you are heading out on your vacation in Copalis Beach area. I can tell you there aren't many markets in that area. I took it upon myself to send you off with enough food for a few days along with a bottle of Tom's wine to remember us by."

Elaine and Lou got up and hugged her and kissed her gently on both sides of her cheeks. Together they looked deeply in her eyes and said in unison, "We will never forget you dear Mama Maria."

"Tom, I took the liberty of having the food put into the helicopter so you can leave here knowing these young ladies will not starve."

"Until we see you again," Lou and Elaine said, blowing her a kiss.

Antonio said, "You know it's funny how you two speak the same thing at the same time sometimes."

"Yes, we have practiced this our whole lives," Elaine said laughingly. They held each other's hands and walked together to the helicopter.

When they landed at Francisco's everyone was sad to say goodbye. Antonio said, "We will call you and see if we can make arrangements to see you on the fourth. It's a yearly event here with everyone in town attending. First there is the parade, then picnics followed by evening fireworks on the beach. I am thinking of giving my staff a three-day vacation, with pay of course. Tom and I have earned a few days off, also."

"Call us!" The girls said in unison.

"That's the plan," Antonio said.

"We haven't had this much fun in I can't say how long," Lou said.

Well, as they hugged the girls and they carried the food baskets to the Rover, Antonio looked at Elaine and said, "Aren't you going to check out the car to see if the coast is clear?"

Elaine said, "How did you know? No, never mind, I already know," Elaine winked at Antonio and said softly, "Until we meet again."

"You can say that again sweet thing; we certainly will meet again," Antonio stated as a fact and not just words.

Tom, on the other hand, was holding Lou so tight, one might wonder if he would break something. As he kissed her, he said, "I wish today would never end."

The girls got settled in the car and said their final goodbyes.

Elaine and Lou waved and headed for the exit of the parking area. Elaine pressed the home button and said, "Inform Bill we are headed to Copalis Beach and the cottage. Please put the Rover in fast mode and notify the highway patrol." She then turned left toward the highway.

Lou was the first to break the silence in the car and told Elaine that TIA told her things were heating up in Copalis Beach and she was needed there sooner than later. "Say no more Sis, we will soon have the okay from TIA and the highway patrol to move at warp speed. We'll only stop for coffee at drive-thrus. It's not too far to Copalis Beach and I don't think we will need gas as our tank is full."

A flash on the dashboard with a message that read, "*All clear to put Rover into fast mode. All concerned have been notified. God speed you two.*" Elaine looked at Lou and suggested she take one of her power naps as everything was under control. "This baby can practically drive itself," Elaine said. Elaine put on her earphones so that any new messages would go directly to her and Lou could have her daydreams in silence. I still marvel at how all traffic remains over to the right and we are allowed to fly by. Elaine passed several highway patrol cars and as she passed, they flashed their headlights at her that it was clear to go.

They stayed on the 109 until they hit Ocean City. The dashboard indicated a right turn onto Copalis Beach road. A few miles down the road an arrow indicated they had arrived at the cottage. Elaine turned into a long dirt driveway. Behind the cottage was a garage, so they pulled in next to it. They had a set of keys and as they got out of the car, motion lights came on to help navigate their way to the cottage door.

Elaine said with a surprise in her voice, "I thought we were going to be roughing it. This is a great looking cottage. Nicely maintained, at least on the outside."

Lou said, "Hope it's that way inside. My friend hasn't been here in a while. But he assured me he would have it cleaned and ready for our arrival." They unlocked the door and headed into what appeared to be the great room.

Elaine set her things down out of the way and said, "Check out the rest of the cottage, Lou. I will bring in the rest of our things. I'll put the baskets Mama Maria gave us in the kitchen and you can put them away while I take the rest of the stuff into the bedrooms."

It did not take long for Elaine to have everything in their respective rooms and she could see Lou had put everything away in the kitchen. Lou said, "I have to contact TIA and see if they have more information for tomorrow."

Elaine said, "I have to make a few calls myself. I will make mine while I'm in the kitchen making coffee and setting the table for dinner."

Lou said, "When I get through with my calls, I'll put out the box of food from Mama Maria that's marked, 'eat upon arrival.'

There is also a small box for the stove top marked 'dessert.' Warmed-up and serve."

Both Elaine and Lou called their handlers and let them know they arrived safely and would be ready for an early start in the morning. Evidently, they both had things to take care of in the morning as both received more instructions.

Elaine looked around the cottage and when Lou was ready, they both checked out what they were about to eat. There was a fresh garden salad, home-made rolls, fresh churned butter and Mama Maria's eggplant parmesan with spaghetti in a marinara tomato sauce. For dessert was a deep-dish apple pie. The girls looked at each other and smiled. They couldn't wait to dig in.

After dinner, Lou was thinking about going to the agency office in Ocean Shores in the morning. Elaine was thinking about calling Carol the roomie to ask if she knew the whereabouts of her roommate. Both Lou and Elaine were expecting packages from TIA. Elaine was expecting her package tonight at 10:00 p.m. On the back porch by the BBQ, Lou was going over the information she had previously received about agent Diane Lane. Facts: Diane is on vacation to enjoy the Fourth of July in Ocean Shores, Washington. While there she got one of her hunches or what Lou thinks, a gut feeling something is about to happen or has already.

Lou will pick up her package tomorrow morning at the agency. Lou would like to know if there are any other agents in town as she would like to get together with them and share information.

Unknown to Lou and Elaine, Nanny and Harry are already in Ocean Shores staying at the Indian casino. They checked the cottage before the girl's arrival and Harry delivered Lou's transportation, parking it in the garage.

# Chapter 21

Earlier in the week, TIA contacted the semi-retired Ms. Brown and Harry Harrison at the girls Malibu California estate. They were instructed to get on a plane going to Aberdeen, Washington. Harry was to pick up a car that would be waiting for him at the airport when they landed. The car was for Lou to drive while in Copalis Beach. Harry was to drive it to the cottage and park it in the garage on the premises.

Both Ms. Brown and Mr. Harrison were regarded as excellent agents, who specialized in being able to disguise themselves so well that acquaintances and other agents wouldn't be able to recognize them. The phone number of the Indian casino would be in the package and he was to call the manager to send a car to pick them up; ask to speak to the manager. Once in disguise they were never to be seen together, if possible. They were to exit and return to their suite through the back entrance of the casino. Unfortunately, they also would not be allowed room service or a maid. This was to protect their identities.

TIA also mentioned it had come to their attention that for some reason there were several secret agents from other European agencies in the area. There are also three of our top agents (all women) who will be residing in the casino for the Fourth of July celebrations.

TIA told them: "You will each be posing as employees of local establishments as cover. The only time anyone will see Harry is when he picks up the package with their new ID's." They were reminded that they have to look different enough to fool Lou and Elaine as they would be eating at the casino often. Diane Lane would also see the girls often at Ace Hardware as it has everything they might need while at the cottage.

Elaine and Lou were watching the local news channel when Elaine realized the lights outside went on and off. Must be the delivery of the package. Elaine excused herself and went to the back porch and lifted the lid on the BBQ. There it was with a cover that had printed on it "charcoal." *Brrr it is cold here in Copalis Beach*, Elaine thought.

She went back in through the laundry room and into the kitchen. She asked Lou in a loud voice, "Do you want some more wine or anything while I am in the kitchen?"

"Yes, thank you but no wine; however, a cup of herbal tea would hit the spot. I'll be going to bed early and can't wait to get under those comforters. This place is chilly and damp."

Elaine said, "Turn up the thermostat in the hall just outside your bedroom, Lou. We are so used to being waited on hand and foot that just turning on the heat is like roughing it to us."

Lou laughed out loud and said, "Leave it to you to zing me."
She took two cups of tea into the tv room and they watched the
end of the local news and then headed for bed. "Leave the light
on in the hall so if you need something in the middle of the night
or have to turn up the heat, you will not fall on the steps that lead
to the tv room."

Elaine went to her bedroom and opened the package. It included
Carol's cell phone number (the missing student's roommate).
There was a typed note that said:

> *We figure it will take you about one day to wrap
> up this case of the missing student if she is alive
> and well. If you find her and talk to her, impress
> on her the fact that her parents are concerned
> that they haven't heard from her in a week or so.
> If for no other reason than making Carol's
> parents relieved that they did nothing wrong by
> taking her on this trip. Be sure and tell the girls
> to notify the office whenever they planned to
> leave on any trip in the future. For all they know
> their parents could have had an emergency and
> needed to reach them.*

Elaine hoped she would be found safe and sound and if all went
well, she would have time to walk around town and explore. She
would make sure to wear her running shoes with the hopes of

having a run. It had been a while since she had had any exercise. *I can run on the beach and plan on where we can see the fireworks to the best advantage. I will also find a store where we can purchase warmer clothes. Now that I have my day planned for tomorrow I can shower and go to sleep, praying all goes well in Ocean Shores,* she thought.

Just before turning out the lights, Elaine perused both of her case files. Elaine wondered if it was her imagination or did the photos of the jewelry the serial killer had given the women looked familiar. *I will have to check further after I run down the missing student from Arizona and hopefully find her safe and enjoying her spring break.*

Meanwhile, Lou talked to her handler and he said they hadn't heard from Diane Lane in days. Lou was hoping she would find out more once she got to the agency office in the morning.

As cold as it is in Copalis Beach, the cottage was warm and both Lou and Elaine slept in. They got up around 8:00 a.m. Elaine did her exercises and at 8:30 a.m. called Carol on her cell. She answered on the first ring. "Hello," she said.

Elaine said, "Is this Carol from the University of Arizona?"

She said, "Yes, who am I speaking to?"

"My name is Elaine and I understand from the university office that you went on spring break with your parents. I'm trying to get in touch with your roommate. Her parents haven't heard from her lately and I was wondering if you knew where she went on spring break?"

Carol was happy to say, "No worries, she is with me and my parents. We have been driving around the countryside in our RV. We've been enjoying all the shops, restaurants, and the ocean beaches. We checked out the fabulous library in the area and did you know you could get a box full of books for a donation of three dollars. What a steal. We bought two boxes of books for us to read while we are on the road back to the university."

Elaine thought, *My, she certainly is bubbly this early in the morning.* Elaine said, "I promised Mary Ann's parents I would contact her and talk to her as soon as I found her. Do you think all of you including your parents can meet me at the local bistro for breakfast? If it's okay with everyone, please have Mary Ann call me to confirm the place and time, my number is on your cell phone."

Carol said, "I'll ask Mary Ann to call you back. Thanks for checking on us here. Oh, just a heads up, Mary Ann and I can't wait for the Fourth of July on the beach but we may not be able to watch the fireworks from the beach as the fog is supposed to start rolling in late afternoon."

Elaine said, "Thanks for the information. I will wait for Mary Ann's call. See you soon I hope; bye for now."

Lou came out into the kitchen and asked if the coffee was made.

Elaine quipped, "What do you think, Sis? I have to have a cup before I do my exercises."

Lou took a cup and put toast in the toaster. "This should hold us over until we go to eat. TIA told me we should try out the Indian casino restaurant on the right-hand side of the main road to Ocean Shores."

"Sounds good," Elaine said.

Lou asked, "What do you want on your toast? Oh, forget it I'll put jam and butter on the table and you can do it yourself as you are always saying we are roughing it. TIA said there is a car in the garage for me to drive while I'm working. All I can say is I hope it is not a Range Rover. That car is nice but not quite me!"

Elaine said, "I think they know you well enough to give you a safe, good looking, tourist style car. No one in their right mind would give you a rough-it type car."

No one is aware that Harry and Nanny are in the Ocean Shores area. They were called out of their so-called retirement because of all the activity in the area. TIA is aware that agents from all over different parts of the world were brought to Ocean Shores but not sure of the reason.

Harry went into the manager's office showed him his ID and picked up the package of instructions. The manager gave him their suite number.

Harry and Nanny went to the back of the casino checking the exits they would need. Each of them had a key that opened their suite and the back door exits.

The keys they were given were another one of the goodies that are secured and untraceable even to machines and tracing equipment. If they had to go through airport screening, nothing would show up. For more sophisticated and newly released technical screen machines, there is a certain capability incorporated in their equipment... TIA has contracts with the manufacturers, so if one of their agents show up with a certain code they would be allowed a free pass with the knowledge they were legally entering that country.

They went up to their suite and Nanny sat down while Harry fixed them a cocktail. Nanny said, "Thanks Harry, this is just what I needed. It has been some whirlwind trip so far."

Harry agreed and said, "That Hyundai Sonata is going to be a surprise to Lou when she opens the garage. I think we should open the package and see what we are supposed to do."

Nanny opened the package and the first thing they read was:

> *Please check the closet. Under the extra pillows you will find all the equipment you will need while you are working, you're top secret undercover assignments. First Ms. Brown you will be working at Ace Hardware in Ocean Shores as a clerk/checkout clerk, you do whatever you feel is necessary not to be recognized. Harry you will work at the casino as a waiter. Full disguise at all times. Please do not be seen talking to each other at any time. That is why you both have special keys and there will be no maid service, we are sorry about that. You can have room service but have them knock and leave it outside your suite. When finished, just leave the empty dishes outside your door and they will be picked up.*

# Chapter 22

Elaine looked at Lou and suggested they check out the garage. They used the keypad on the outside of the garage (combination was in Lou's package). There was a four door Hyundai Sonata. Lou was happy and said to Elaine that this car has all the bells and whistles, leather interior, completely bulletproof, and dashboard amenities that the Rover has with the exception of the fast-tracking speed system.

Elaine laughed and said, "It's super with the exception you are usually chauffeured around; so my dear Sis, be sure and set the GPS to and from the cottage. It will save you a lot of angst. If you can't find an address, store or something, just press that button and ask your question and it will answer. You might find it's fun to be in charge of your car and not just your gentlemen friends."

Elaine had a smile on her face because she could read Lou's mind without saying a word.

Lou said, "Now, now, Sis. Do I detect some envy?"

Elaine looked at Lou and said, "In your dreams, Sis! I'm happy with my choice in society doing what I'm good at. Believe me, I couldn't do what you have to do...being eye candy when your IQ is double what your escorts have."

Lou said, "Let's each of us take our cars and go to the Indian casino for breakfast."

"Sounds good. You follow me so you can get used to your car. Drive to the 'Y' in the road and keep left for a few miles. There will be a large sign for the casino indicating a right turn," Elaine said.

They followed the signs to the casino and pulled up as close to the front entrance as they could get, parking next to each other. Before going into the casino, they made sure their cars were secure.

Lou and Elaine saw the cafe as they entered. They made their way to the cafe where a woman asked, "Will you be two or more for breakfast this morning?"

"Just the two of us please," Lou said.

The woman said, "Follow me. We have a booth by the window with a beautiful view of the ocean."

Harry saw them as the woman said, "Your waiter is Richard and he will be happy to take your order. If you have any questions about our town, just ask him. We take pride in all the things our town has to offer."

Harry sporting a well-groomed beard and mustache put his white towel over his right arm as they did in England, stood up straight and went over to get their order. He filled their water glasses and in his best accent asked, "Would you like coffee, tea or juice to start my ladies?"

Lou said, "We would like strong hot coffee please."

He smiled and said, "One moment please." He walked to his service station and returned with a carafe of hot coffee. He placed different flavored coffee creams, milk, sugar and honey on the side. He walked away to serve a table with four people. They seemed to be regulars as they said, "Hi Richard! When you get a chance, we will have our regular order."

Richard said, "I'll place your order now." Richard came back and took their order.

Lou said, "We shall make it easy and both of us will have the eggs benedict with home fries on the side."

He said, "A good choice," and walked away.

Shortly, Richard brought a tray with their orders and placed on the table. He then picked up the carafe and filled up their coffee mugs. He asked, "Do wish anything else, ladies?"

Lou and Elaine shook their heads. Elaine said, "Everything looks wonderful, thank you!"

He smiled and turned to check on his other tables.

Elaine and Lou consumed their food and refilled their coffee cups and waited for their check. Lou said she would pick up the tab and leave Richard a really good tip. Elaine took offense and said, "What the heck do you think I do when I travel girl? I have been around the world and back, so to speak, and know what is right and wrong when it comes to tipping."

Lou shrugged.

"By the way I hope to close my other case sometime this week. I hope yours goes fast as well," said Elaine.

Lou mentioned, "I have a couple of meetings to attend. Why don't we get together at the cottage for dinner? I'll pick-up a couple of grocery items and we can finish up Mama Maria leftovers."

"Now Lou, do you think you can get around town and find your way back to the cottage?" Elaine said.

"You bet, Sis. I'll go to the local real estate office and pick up two maps of Ocean Shores and the surrounding area, but then I can always use my GPS in my car."

Richard came by and placed the check on the table. Lou always used cash when she was on a case, less explanation, etc. To the home office. They both got up and walked towards the exit. The woman at the front desk said in a happy voice, "Thank you and please come again."

The doors unlocked and the girls got into their respective cars. They both left the casino parking lot, each taking a different route to attend their specific business.

On Elaine's way downtown, she saw some woodcarvers with their goods for sale. She decided to stop and park to look at their craftsmanship.

She took a couple of photos as tourists often do as she blended in with the crowd. She asked questions about Ocean Shores and the Fourth of July fireworks from different vendors. They all had the same news, just as Carol had told her. There might be fog rolling in so they would be lucky if they would be able to see the fireworks.

Elaine walked back to her car; as Elaine got in, her cell phone rang. It was Mary Ann and she said, "Hello, Elaine, this is Mary

Ann. I'm sorry you had to search for me because I didn't call my folks, but I wasn't even sure they knew it was spring break. Since I'm of age, so to speak, I didn't think I had to check-in. I can see why they might have started to worry if they called the university and found out I wasn't there. They rarely call and getting to go somewhere in an RV with Carol was exciting to me. We've had so much fun. Being on the road and able to walk around, laugh, read and just feel free for the first time since I started university, I completely forgot they might call. If they had called my cell, all their worries would have been unnecessary."

Elaine said she totally understood and asked if she could take all of them out for breakfast, say tomorrow if everyone is free. "We can go to The Bistro in Ocean Shores. You or Carol can call me with the time you'd like to meet."

Elaine drove out onto the road towards Ocean Shores. She stopped to fill-up with gas and asked the attendant if she could suggest where she might purchase some warmer clothes. The women suggested Ace Hardware.

As she pulled into the Ace Hardware parking lot, her cell began to ring. It was Carol and she said they would all be pleased to meet her at the bistro around 9:00 a.m. tomorrow morning. Elaine told her she was looking forward to it and that she would be wearing a red cap. Also, whoever arrived first should get a table for five.

Having parked, she made her way into Ace Hardware. Elaine was surprised to see that this store was not like the ones she saw in Arizona or California. This one was large, had everything the other stores had, plus it was a cross between Sam's Club and Costco. She went to the back of the store and checked out the winter clothing. Elaine found a warm black lined windbreaker with a hood, a woolen scarf, gloves, and a red stocking cap. The cap covered her ears and fit her really well.

The store was filled with lots of locals as well as tourists. The check-out line was long but moved along quickly. When you got to the front of the line you could see why as there were three cashiers. All of them had smiles on their faces and you felt as though you knew them. Elaine had a lovely woman named Rose. She had red hair and her accent was straight out of Ireland. Elaine wondered how long she had been in America. She certainly made people feel special. Elaine paid her and thanked her with a smile and proceeded to walk to the car.

The Rover door unlocked and she put her things in the back seat. She realized she might need a mid-morning snack. Looking up the street she noticed a nondescript restaurant with lots of cars in front and back. This place must be good Elaine thought considering all of the vehicles lined-up in the parking lot.

Elaine sat down and decided to have a garden salad, half a chicken sandwich, a cup of coffee, and a glass of water. She decided she would then go for a run further up the road to check out the library that the students were so gunned up about.

It was a quaint library where you could trade books or you could purchase them. The volunteers were very welcoming, extending lovely hospitality, which was surely the reason the library was such a success.

Elaine went into the room where Carol said they could buy a box of books for three dollars. They had a colorful cashbox for you to put your money in. Elaine noticed that the library didn't need to worry about people not paying as people were dropping money into the box even if they didn't purchase a book.

While perusing books in the fiction section of the library, Elaine found a book on the back roads of Washington. Elaine put a ten-dollar bill into the box and a man watching her said, "Oh, that is way too much." Elaine thanked him and she could see he was, if you'll excuse the expression, "not well healed." She suggested, "Please select a couple of books on me."

He look surprised and asked, "Really, you're not kidding, are you?"

Elaine smiled and said, "No, let's just say I am paying it forward." He smiled and one would think I had given him the world.

He said with enthusiasm, "I come in almost every day. I sit and read, then when it's closing time, I place the book I'm reading in an area where no one would look for it."

"Now!" He said with a great big smile, "I will take it home and finish it then return it for another. Again ma'am, thank you so much for your kindness."

Elaine left with a book and her heart was full as well. She looked up and said under her breath, "Thank you, God. This is going to be a really great day." Elaine got into her Rover and drove to the center of town where she decided to check out the visitors' center and do some walking.

Elaine started to enter the visitors' center and through the open doors she noticed there were lots of men in suits and ties walking around with refreshments in their hands. She noticed they, for the most part, were from all areas of the world and many had interpreters.

A woman sitting at a table caught her eye and motioned for Elaine to come over. Elaine stood up and asked if she could help with something. Elaine smiled and asked if this was the visitors center where she might get information on Ocean Shores including walking areas. The woman profusely apologized and said, "I'm very sorry, not today as this is a three day meeting that is by invitation only. If you could come back then, I certainly will be able to assist you."

Elaine then motioned to a man who was definitely not a guest but a security guard. Her agent training took over and she acted like a tourist and said to her, "No worries, if I can't get a map from a realtor's office, I will see you in a few days. Thanks again."

Elaine headed toward the beach. *With all those foreigners in town, I think I will check some of the resorts close by to see if they are full and if so ask where I might get a room*, she thought.

Elaine stopped in at the first resort she came across. She asked the desk clerk if there were any rooms available for the Fourth of July. The desk clerk said, "Well that will probably be an impossibility as we and most of the local resort hotels are booked solid for about two years. There is a special conference going on and they booked a package deal just for them. You could try at the casino as they might have something and you can see the fireworks from there if the weather stays clear."

*Well,* Elaine thought, *there's something going on in this little town that needs to be looked into. I will go back to the cottage and ask TIA if it knows about this European conference/seminar.*

It was an easy drive back to Copalis Road and the cottage was easy to find in the daylight hours. *I know Lou will spot this place when she comes home.*

Elaine parked in the back of the cottage near the garage but far enough away so Lou could park inside the garage or next to the Rover. She thought: *This cottage is safe with all the security around the area. I noticed there were highway patrols in force on a lot of back roads that I feel would not normally be patrolled. Another thing to mention to Bill/TIA.*

*I'll call Bill after I take my shower and freshen up. Knowing Bill, he will want to know all about my case and what I think of everything. Also, he will probably ask if Lou likes living on the wild side.*

*Lou should be heading home soon, I think. I hope she got the information she needs to proceed with her case. Lou will have to have breakfast alone tomorrow as I hope to close my case of the missing Arizona university student. I will take photos to send to Bill, with all four of them standing in front of the RV, which if I take the photo correctly will show the license number, just in case something unforeseen happens on their way back to Arizona and their dorm.*

Lou honked as she turned onto the driveway and pulled back near the garage and parked next to the Rover. Lou had also gone to Ace Hardware and picked up some warm clothes along with several other things. Elaine said to Lou when she walked in with several bundles of purchases, "I see you found Ace Hardware and found everything to help keep you warm when you are out and about."

Lou said, "I sure did, it's a great store. Now I have to call my handler and tell him what I found out today."

Elaine said, "Yes, our work is never done. I have to call Bill and take care of business, too."

Lou said, "I need to freshen up and then we can have the Caesar salad I brought, which should go well with Mama Marias' left-overs. I also have to read the package I picked up at the agency and read it before I call TIA."

"How was your drive back to the cottage, Lou? Did you have any trouble finding your way?" Elaine asked.

Lou said, "There was no problem at all, I just spoke to the dashboard and requested they direct me to the cottage. It was funny, along with verbal directions, the dash would flash showing me when there were highway patrol cars nearby. I sure would hate to get a ticket. I would never stop hearing about it from the accounting department. They have more patrols in this area than all of Aberdeen. Must be because of all the tourists in town for the Fourth of July celebrations."

"Go and freshen up and we can talk about that while we eat," Elaine suggested.

Elaine's cell rang: it was Antonio calling. *Well, maybe he is coming up for the Fourth*, she hoped. Elaine answered softly, "Well, hello stranger; what's on your mind?"

Antonio proceeded to tell her that they would be taking a few days off and had made arrangements for Tom to fly them to Ocean Shores. "We'll land at the heliport at the casino where they will have a car waiting for us."

"That's so great!" Elaine said. Elaine thought, *Darn, I did it again*, saying what she was thinking instead of what Lou does. Lou would have said something like, "How do you know I am available?" *Oh well, I think Antonio knows I was expecting his call.*

# Chapter 23

Antonio asked, "What's happening in your little town. Is it dull or exciting? Have you closed your case or will I have to see the sights by myself? Tom will call Lou, so don't tell her he is going to call. Keep her waiting. If I'm correct, she is used to keeping friends waiting."

Elaine laughed and said, "I know you know me somewhat; however, I didn't know you observed Lou and critiqued her as well."

"I've closed my case but believe I've come across something strange." Antonio queried, "And what's that sweet thing?"

Elaine thought for a minute about telling him what she observed: *Considering his previous position in Europe, maybe he could give me a different perspective on this strange situation.*

Elaine continued: "I did, just by chance come across something strange, at least to me when I went to the tourist center for information. The doors were open, so I walked in and there were men dressed in suits and ties, but even more questionable was they were from all over the world, some with interpreters. A woman saw me and motioned me to come to her desk. She said the facility was booked for a private seminar and by invitation only and that she was sorry but couldn't help me at that time.

She then motioned for a man that was standing nearby and requested I be shown out. I went immediately into my tourist mode so she didn't realize I noticed anything strange. After I was escorted out, I went down the road to one of the resorts to see if I could find out what was going on. The concierge said there was a group that had booked all the rooms for two years in the local area as well as a center down the road for a conference. Well, which is it a seminar or conference?"

Because of Antonio's previous business in Europe, and the fact he never closed his contacts and business associates, he was sent an invitation to attend a conference in Ocean Shores but had brushed it off as something he wasn't interested in. Now, he was thinking it was more to it than he had thought. Antonio said: "Well, what do you know? I was invited to such a conference. I never thought much about it. I still have the invitation filed away. I believe Tom received an invite as well. Hmmm, what say we come earlier? We can close earlier and head your way tomorrow. Between you and I, we can have fun and we might unearth something America isn't supposed to know. I haven't had this much fun to think about in years. Are you game?"

Elaine said if she closed her case tomorrow, she'd be happy to check it out."

Antonio said, "I'll book our reservations at the casino and call you with our itinerary."

176

Elaine quickly said, "Antonio, I hear Lou coming down the hall. I'll anxiously wait for your next call."

He said softly and in a sexy voice, "Till then, my dear."

"I don't know if you ever saw old movies about Mr. And Mrs. North. That's who we could be. Check it out," Elaine said. Mr. And Mrs. North was a 1952 tv series about a husband and wife who were amateur sleuths who tried to solve crimes before the police did.

Antonio said, "I will. Till then, my love. Stay safe."

A chill went through her as she hung up.

Lou entered the room and looked at Elaine and said, "You're blushing and I'm sure you weren't talking to Bill. Come on Sis, who were you talking to?"

"That's for me to know and you to find out," Elaine said. She added, "Let's have dinner, Lou. You can set the table and I'll get everything else ready. Do you want me to make coffee?"

"Sounds good to me, as I haven't had coffee since this morning," Lou said.

Elaine said, "Oh, speaking of morning, I have to leave early for a breakfast meeting so you will have to have breakfast on your own."

"Don't worry about me. I'm tied up with meetings as well," Lou said.

Elaine said to Lou, "Was there anything you noticed in Ocean Shores today that seemed unusual?"

"Like what?" Lou asked.

"I'm not sure, I can't seem to put my finger on it, but I did notice there were a lot of foreigners in town. I didn't know the Fourth of July in Ocean Shores was so popular in Europe."

Lou said, "Where were you that you encountered them? Were they from France, Italy or Germany?"

Elain said, "Many more countries than that and they had interpreters telling them what was going on, etc."

Lou said frowning, "I think we should inform both our handlers and ask them why."

"I'll do that and let you know what Bill thinks," Elaine stated.

Lou said, "I'll do the same. You may have stumbled onto something."

Elaine said, "My feelings exactly." They cleared up the dinner dishes and agreed they would make their respective calls to their handlers and then meet back for the evening news on tv.

Elaine called TIA and Bill answered: "Come on, come on... Hi, there Elaine. What's new in your part of town? Hope you have good news for me."

Elaine answered, "I do. I talked with Mary Ann and am following up by taking all four of them to breakfast tomorrow. I will take a couple of photos of Mary Ann, Carol and her parents standing by their RV. I'll be sure to include the license plate number. If I had a tracker, I could put one on the RV."

With that Bill said, "Stop at the agency and ask for your package."

Elaine cautiously said to Bill: "I have something I want to run by you. It may sound crazy to you but I guess I was in 'agent mode' today when I went into the tourist center to get a map of the local running paths and stores. The doors were open and I noticed many foreigners inside, as well as interpreters. The woman at the desk told me it was a private seminar and she couldn't help me at that time and then I was promptly escorted out. This seemed very odd, being escorted out. So, I walked down toward the beach where there are lots of resorts. I know you can learn a lot from staff at hotels as there's usually a lot of gossip that goes on in those establishments. I was told that the hotels have been booked for about two years for a conference at the center. Being escorted out of the information center, rooms being booked in advance for two years, men in suits and ties and from all over the world smells like dead fish to me. What say you Bill? Can you check this out for me so I can be sure the locals are safe? My friend Antonio and his side kick Tom are flying here and will be staying at the Indian casino. You know I told you he said his profession before he retired was a man that worked the back roads of Europe. I told him what I saw and he said he thought that was odd and that he received an invitation, as did Tom to this particular conference. He suggested we might just go and see just what is really happening. Even suggested that it might be something that they don't want America to know about."

Bill said: "Well kiddo, TIA is aware there are too many foreign agents in that area and wondered what was up. You just might have stumbled onto a way of finding out. I'll ask here what they think of your suggestion. Having a way to get into a conference by invitation only suggests you have the opportunity. Since you will be in good hands and will be safe, not saying you are not capable of taking care of yourself, but with Antonio there, I would say between the two of you, if indeed something is amiss, you will certainly be able to find out what. Does Antonio know you speak lots of languages?"

"No, but he will. Antonio and I can play like the old tv series, Mr. And Mrs. North," Elaine said.

Bill laughed and said, "I think you need to get out more and keep up with the times or at least more current spy series/movies. However, you just might have something there."

Elaine said, "There are an abundance of local highway patrol cars all over Ocean Shores. Even as far out as where our cottage is. Lou noticed it as well. She seems to feel the same way I do and finds this all very strange. Her friend Tom is coming with Antonio and he also received an invitation to this conference. If that is a help. Let me know what is up and any rumors you may hear about. I will do the same," Elaine said.

Elaine went into the kitchen and Lou was there getting coffee. "Hey Sis, did you get hold of the office? Is everything going okay?"

Lou said, "I have my work cut out for me starting tomorrow. One last cup of coffee for both of us as we watch the news and then try and get a good night's sleep. I think we both have to be fresh as daisies in the morning."

"Anything new tonight?" Elaine asked.

Lou answered, "Nothing new I need to mention. Just case work and it includes searching the area, probably more walking and phone calls. With luck and if all goes well, I can finish my case in a day or so and then you and I can have a good time."

"I'm ready for that!" Elaine said.

"I told the company about what we uncovered and I assume you did also," Lou said.

"Yup, I informed them and Bill was glad to hear about what we came up with and told me to keep my/our eyes open. Well, it's that time Lou... I have to get my beauty rest and get up early to take care of business in the morning. I want to run and get something I will need before I stop for breakfast. You play it safe, Lou, and call me if you come into anything questionable."

They both headed to turn in for the night. *Hopefully all will go well tomorrow and make the day go by fast*, they both thought.

Elaine slept well, got up, showered and made fresh coffee. Elaine planned her morning: *I'll go for a run and then stop in at the agency to pick up my package. I'll head for the restaurant and take the promised pictures. Then I think I may go by where the conference is being held. Maybe take a few photos of the license plates as they may come in handy. With the woodcarvers and other vendors displaying their work in the lot next to the center, I will just appear as a happy tourist.*

Elaine left and headed for the agency to pick up the transmitter and notes that might be in the package. *I always enjoy checking into the local agency offices*, she thought. She wore her red hat, new jacket, and gloves. She put on her sunglasses and put her ID card in her inside pocket.

Her GPS system directed her right to the agency. She went in and showed her ID, picked up her package, and got in the Rover. She drove across the parking lot and onto the main road. She drove a block and turned in to park at the restaurant. She opened the envelope, pulled out her instructions and a small transmitter. Bill had instructions as to where on the RV would be the best place to install it. He said there was a goodie inside the transmitter that TIA can listen in on the conversation should it become necessary.

Elaine put the transmitter inside her glove so she would have easy access and be able to make a quick installation. When she pulled into the parking lot of the bistro there was an RV parked taking up two spaces. That must be the one as it was the only RV in the parking area. She pulled in beside it, on the far side not facing the restaurant window. She thought: *I'll have to go in, introduce myself and then excuse myself, telling them I have to make sure I locked my car doors. Then I'll go to the RV and install the transmitter and return to the restaurant.*

Elaine walked in and was immediately recognized by her red hat. She made her introductions and then excused herself. Installing the transmitter was easier than she thought. She returned to the bistro and Carol came over and said, "We can order at the front and they bring everything to our table."

The glass cases were full of homemade breads, rolls, muffins, sweet and savory pastries and donuts. Everything looked so fresh. Elaine walked up to the counter and said to put the four orders in front of her on her tab. She would pay for theirs.

Elaine and Carol talked about the trip and what they had been doing here. Elaine said she went to the library and got a book. She casually asked what route they would be taking to return to Arizona. She had touched her maroon stone on her bracelet so it records voices and the routes one will take. When finished, she just touched it twice and it stopped recording. The recording went directly to TIA and they would be able to see if they deviate from their route.

*It's hard to believe that Mary Ann may still be in danger; however, being from Germany and a dignitary's daughter, we can't take a chance of her being kidnapped while she is here or on the way back to Arizona. Never mind there are people here in Ocean Shores from all over the world and we don't know why. It is just too coincidental, I think. I hope I am wrong*, Elaine thought.

## Chapter 24

Lou was up and about, had her coffee, and dressed for cold weather. She locked up the house and got into her car and headed out to work on her case. She went to the agency and asked if they came up with the phone numbers of the agents here in Ocean Shores and their addresses so she could get together with them to exchange information. It was a new woman in the office and she assumed Lou was expecting this information. She went on her computer, found the information, and printed it out. *What a break*, Lou thought.

She left the agency saying, "Thanks, just what I needed; you're the greatest!" She turned to get out quickly before the woman that runs the agency came back. "Whew, did I get a break just then or what! I hope she doesn't get in trouble for giving out this information," Lou said under her breath. She got into her car and drove out of the parking lot turned left and drove into the roundabout staying in the left lane and turned right on the road to have breakfast at the restaurant just down from Ace Hardware.

She took out her cell and called her handler, Rich. She asked him, "What name might Diane be using when she went to the agency here? I acquired a list of agents that are here in the area." Now she has to find Diane and if she is under a different name try to locate her on that list.

Rich said, "Check to see if there is a person under the name of D. Johnson."

"Will do Rich. Do you have an update from Diane or any news from her?" Lou asked.

"No, Lou we haven't heard from her lately. If you make contact with her, inform her she must contact TIA immediately. Let her know she must not leave a message but speak directly to her handler, as there are some serious problems," Rich said.

Lou said to Rich, "Will do!"

Lou went into the restaurant, sat down at a small table for two, and tilted the other chair letting everyone to know the table was taken. The waiter went to give her a menu, but she piped up, "I'll have two eggs over easy, with crisp bacon, sourdough toast, and hot coffee."

"You got it lady," he said and walked toward his station to put the order into the computer. He came back and poured her a cup of hot coffee.

She took out the list of agents which was two pages long. Knowing TIA doesn't have that many agents in one place at one time the girl must have printed every agent in town, not just the ones from TIA.

Lou made a note to tell Rich about the list and send a copy to him. TIA will want to investigate where those agents not affiliated with TIA are from. This list might have something to do with what Elaine found out when she went to the tourist center yesterday. Elaine and Lou's minds were in sync and there was trouble in paradise.

The waiter came with Lou's breakfast, filled her coffee cup, and asked if there was anything she needed. "No thank you. This looks so good and I can't wait to taste it," she replied.

She checked the list for D. Johnson or Diane Lane as she ate her food. *Oh boy, what luck. There is a phone number and address for D. Johnson.*

Lou underlined D. Johnson on the list, finished her meal and paid the check. She got up and happily went to her car. The door unlocked as she walked next to it and once she was in the driver's seat, the doors locked automatically.

She took out her cell and called D. Johnson. She let it ring four times and was about to hang up when a voice on the other end of the phone said, "Hello!"

Lou said, "I hope I have the correct phone number for D. Johnson. Is this Diane?"

Diane said, "How did you get this phone number? Do I know you?"

Lou replied, "It's Lou, we know each other, and I got your address and phone number from the agency. I'm here visiting the area to view the fireworks. I heard you're on vacation, also."

Diane said, "Oh, hi. What's on your mind?"

Lou said, "Your friend from TIA told me to contact you and we could have coffee and/or have a bite to eat. Maybe you would rather we meet for coffee or a drink somewhere close to where you reside?"

"That sounds good to me. We can meet at the coffee drive through beside the Ace Hardware store. They have an outdoor patio with heaters so we can enjoy the fresh air but stay warm."

Lou said, "Diane, I have news from your friend, shall we meet in fifteen minutes on the patio? I'm driving a Sonata."

Diane said, "Okay, see you there."

Diane and Lou sat at the patio table nearest the heater. "The cold here chills you to the bone, not like California. Diane, I am so glad to see you again. If I recall correctly, the last time we saw each other was in Sweden at the All World Conference?"

"Yes, I remember now. How have you been?" Diane asked.

"Great. Keeping busy as I see you are. Aren't you supposed to be on vacation? What happened to cause you to stop contacting TIA?They are concerned and want you to call them and not leave messages as they need to talk. I think it must be super important. You are the reason I'm here! I was sent to find you."

Diane, while looking around to see if anyone was watching or listening to them, said, "I was here for a vacation and got one of my premonitions that was so strong I couldn't sleep. It has to do with the conference we attended in Sweden. Remember, there were people and not just agents from all over the world. I overheard a conversation between some men and it was something I wasn't supposed to hear. It had to do with an event that was to happen this year. A few weeks ago, I was eating at the casino and saw the same men here. They saw me and evidently recognized me. I pretended I didn't know them. I paid my check and went out to my car. It was then, one of the men followed me out and took down my license plate number. That in itself was a tell-tale sign that something was up. All I remember overhearing was the year this event was to take place, not where or what the event was. I guess they thought I overheard everything they were saying while in Sweden. I called TIA and it rang many times. I was afraid they (the men that recognized me) might try and get me in the parking lot, so I just left a message. Things moved fast for me after that."

Lou said, "What did you do to avoid them?"

"I thought I gave them the slip until I saw I was being followed by two different cars. They tried to fool me as a tag team. I took measures not to go to my place and drove past it. I turned several times, and the car immediately behind me moved on while a similar car picked me up and continued following me. I diverted my route to the roundabout where the first car picked me up again and the other car kept going. I saw Ace Hardware on my right so I made a quick lane change and went into their parking lot and parked by the front door. I know they have good cameras and security on the premises. I got out, turned on the car transmitter so when I came out, I could see if there were any problems. TIA did not alert me; so I am always out of bottled water, so I purchased some and went to the car and used my ankle bracelet to see if it was all clear. The doors unlocked so I knew there wasn't a car or agent within a mile of me. I had a friend that worked at the Purple Pub and so I drove over there and went in. She was working and I asked if she could go on a break as I needed to ask a favor of her. Let me first say she could be my sister; we look so much alike. If we stood next to each other you wouldn't know she wasn't me. I didn't think of that at the time I asked her if she wanted to share her apartment with me. I told her we could save money that way."

"Gosh, that's a good idea Diane. When do you want to move in?" April said.

"Is today too soon?"

"It is ok with me. I live very close to here. Here's the key and address. Maybe we can have dinner tonight?"

Diane went back to her place and packed up her stuff. She wanted to keep the apartment until the end of the month in case it was discovered by any tails. She was sure she was very careful moving into the apartment.

Lou said, "Don't you know you're playing Russian roulette with both of your lives?"

Diane said, "This wasn't a case and I wanted to be sure I was on the right track before I called TIA."

"Well Diane, never mind if you are on the right track or not, you must call TIA and tell them exactly what you told me. It's my feeling something is going on in this town that is way beyond you just being followed. Does April know that you have been followed?"

Diane said, "No, I planned on telling her as soon as I saw her, but she hasn't come home yet."

Diane continued, "I went into her bedroom after I moved in to take back a ring, I loaned her a few weeks ago. It wasn't on her dresser like she said it would be. I tried calling her at work but the manager said she had left already. I'll tell her someone is following me when she gets home."

Lou told her to do it and do it now because what is happening is very dangerous.

They finished their coffee and Diane said not to worry she would check in with TIA and when April got home, she would fill her in also. They said their goodbyes and made plans to meet in a day or so.

Lou took no chances and notified TIA and Rich exactly what Diane had told her. Lou wanted to know was her case over or was there more they wanted her to do?

Rich said he would have to check with the powers that be, but as far as he was concerned, she should be careful and make sure to have her transmitter on twenty-four seven. If she thought she picked up a tail, she should inform him immediately, drive to the Indian casino, go to the café, but by no means leave until she heard back from him.

Rich said he would have Bill call Elaine and tell her to go to the casino and join her. They would put both of their cars on full alert so the area can be checked for problems. He told them not to leave until both of them are called or texted personally.

# Chapter 25

Elaine headed to the casino per Bill's instructions. She pulled in next to Lou's car and texted Bill to let him know she had arrived. *It will be nice to take a break after all the photos I took for his perusal of the cars, drivers, and other people loitering around the conference area*, she thought.

There was a woman she met from Kinderhook, N.Y. They started talking and she took photos of her all over the place. One for her camera and one for her own. That way anyone watching would think they were site seeing together.

There was a woodcarving of a large eagle someone made and it was placed near the entrance of the center. Elaine asked a man that was standing by to take their photo standing alongside of the eagle. First with her friend's camera and then her camera. She asked him to stand back a little so she could get the name of the center; however, what Elaine really wanted was to get a photo of the man that just came out of the center. It was the security guard that had ushered her out of the center the day before. Elaine felt she wouldn't be recognized as she was dressed completely different, wearing sunglasses and her hair down.

The two women walked back to the parking lot where all the people were selling their wares. Elaine said the time had gotten

194

away from her so she would have to leave. She thanked her for her friendship and tales of Kinderhook, N.Y., where she lived and so on. Elaine said goodbye to her friend and went to the Rover and got in and when the car's safety belt went on and the doors locked, the dashboard flashed the all clear to go to the casino.

Elaine sent the photos to Bill before going into the casino. She went to the cafe and found Lou munching on a cheese and fruit plate along with sweet tea. Lou said, "Help yourself to the fruit plate and get something to drink."

Elaine said, "I'll get a glass of cold water with lemon. How did your day go? Did you solve your case?"

Lou said sighing, "I may have gotten in deeper than I thought. Rich is contacting Bill and we will both hear what we have fallen into."

Elaine said, "Oh no, don't include me please, so far I think I fared well today."

Both of the girl's phones rang notifying them in a text about what their next move would be. First line in the text for both Lou and Elaine was: *TIA wants you both to fill each other in on what you both have found out, along with what Diane has come up with in Ocean Shores. You ladies talk it over and work together when necessary. Top secret all the way.The highway patrol has found a dead body of a women wearing Diane's ring. We know it isn't Diane. We will let everyone believe that it is Diane and not her friend April for security purposes.*

Rich told Lou, "Please contact your mother and ask her to forward the photos you took while in Sweden at the World Conference. We'll get a set also. We want you and Elaine to check the photos taken at the conference and compare them against the photos Elaine sent today. We may really have something very serious going on."

Bill called Elaine and said, "We have your case under control as you planned. Hopefully, nothing will go wrong with Mary Ann and her party on their trip back home. That frees both of you to handle this new problem with what is going on at the center. Have you heard from Antonio? Let me know ASAP."

Bill continued, "You can both go back to the cottage where we will send further instructions. They will be placed inside the BBQ just like last time. However, because of the nature of things they'll honk when they enter and leave the driveway. Please stay up to receive it. Be on the lookout for trouble and start carrying a gun from now on."

Lou said to Elaine, "I'll leave the casino first and could you play backup and make sure there are no cars following me? Diane had a tag team following her."

"No problem. I'll send you a message if I think you're being followed. I'll make sure I'm not being tailed as well," Elaine answered.

Lou and Elaine arrived at the cottage without incident. Elaine parked beside the garage and motioned for Lou to park inside the garage. *If they are looking for a Sonata, they won't find one here, whomever they are*, Elaine thought. *I sure hope Antonio calls tonight. I could stand some good news after what Lou and I faced today, and what Diane faces when she gets back to England and that poor murdered girl that was mistaken for Diane. I'll call Bill later when we get the photos and make a comparison. I hope there'll be some men in them that match my photos and/or Lou recognizes some. That may give us a hint as to what these men are doing here. I will be glad to hear when Antonio will arrive and I hope Tom calls Lou.*

Lou came into the TV area and asked, "Wine or coffee, Sis?"

Elaine said, "I'd love a glass of wine. I've had enough coffee today to last through the evening."

"Wine it is, Sis. You seem relieved to be home," Lou said.

"I am and that's because if we can identify any of the men in the photos I took today and compare them to the ones you took in Sweden and we find a match, it may help solve why so many foreigners are here at the same time in an invitation only conference," said Elaine.

Elaine continued, "Bill said to wait up for the package tonight. He also said we were to work together to gather information on why there are so many agents in Ocean Shores. Don't you think it's lucky we're both somewhat free to work on this conference together? Oh, by the way, have you heard from Tom?"

Lou said, "I did but have been so sidetracked with work that I forgot to tell you."

"Well, what did he say?"

"Antonio and Tom will be coming to Ocean Shores today and will stay at the Indian casino. They'll call and make arrangements to see us as soon as they can."

"That's great! Did you know that both Antonio and Tom were invited to that conference? Bill seems to think that may be our way into the conference."

While sipping their wine Lou said, "Diane has been sent back to England for her safety and I believe because she broke protocol by exposing April to danger without April's knowledge."

Elaine said, "If this conference turns out to indeed have the same attendees as the conference in Sweden, then there is most definitely some sort of covert operations in the works. We will need to find out why, when and where this serious top secret plan is to come to fruition."

Lou almost fell asleep when they were watching the evening news, so Elaine suggested that only one of them needed to wait up for the package. Elaine said, "Why don't you go on to bed Lou and I'll stay up? I have some calls to make and I'm expecting a call."

Lou said, "You know Sis, I think I'll take you up on that because I'll need fresh eyes when we go over the photos." With that, Lou went on to bed.

Elaine was thinking about Antonio and just then the phone rang. She picked it up and Antonio said, "Hi, babe. I'm all settled in my suite at the casino and Tom is in his. He told me he spoke to Lou earlier in the evening. I had some business to take care of but now my time is all yours, dear."

Elaine said, "Hi yourself. I'm relaxing and Lou has gone to bed so we can talk. I'd like to know: did you accept the invitation for the conference/seminar or whatever it is?"

Antonio said, "Yes, Tom and I are on their list. Did you get an okay to be my interpreter and do you think that Lou could be Tom's? I talked to him and he would love having her on his arm. I told him this was going to be business and not just another conference."

Elaine said, "Our bosses have given the okay. We need to uncover as much information along with photos but make it look like we are there for fun and games, so to speak. It will be another case for me. I hope you will enjoy being Mr. and Mrs. North."

Antonio replied, "Well, dear, if that is what you want, I think we can manage that undercover, that is." Antonio asked, "Shall we meet for breakfast tomorrow morning in the casino cafe? You pick the time."

Elaine answered, "We'd love to; however, we have to check out some case material in the morning. Let's meet at 10:30 a.m."

Antonio said, "It's a deal. I look forward to seeing you. It seems like forever since I last saw you. Stay safe honey, I don't want anything to happen to you."

"Okay, until tomorrow!" Elaine said softly.

Antonio said, "Wait, dear. Did I say I miss you?"

Elaine said, "I've missed you as well!" And hung up. She thought: *Oh dear, I know I should have played hard to get like Lou but I couldn't pull it off. I can exaggerate stories and untruths when it comes to business, but my personal life (what little I have), I usually always keep things close to my chest. For some reason with Antonio, and I can't seem to put my finger on it, I seem to blurt out exactly what I'm thinking. It's been that way from the moment I first met him.*

A car horn sounded and the outdoor sensor lights went on. Elaine waited for the second horn sound and lights to go off stating they had left. Elaine put on her jacket and with her gun in hand opened the back door to the porch. She checked her surroundings and then looked inside of the BBQ. She picked up the package and noticed a large sized box with her name on it. Before going back into the house, she looked to see that the Rover was still there and that all was okay outside. She went back in and proceeded to open the package. The package held what seemed to be the photos Lou was waiting for along with the printed photos of the film she'd sent Bill of Mary Ann along with a note.

The note said they were confirming the identities of the people Mary Ann was with. With the transmitter she had attached to the RV, they were keeping an eye on any move they make. Also, one of their local contacts were watching their comings and goings while still in Ocean Shores.

Elaine thought, *Then my case of the missing student is over, I guess. Somehow, I won't feel it's over until Mary Ann is in Arizona in her dorm.*

The box that was delivered was from Bill. She opened it anxiously to see what news if any he and his staff had come up with, but then why didn't he just put it in the package she'd just opened up? *Hmm, that's strange.*

She got a knife and opened the box and what a surprise! Inside, she found a designer navy blue business suit in her size and a white silk blouse with a plunging neckline—as well as all the accessories, stockings, shoes, and unmentionables from a designer of lingerie from Paris; enough for a week. *Well, Bill sure knows how to treat a girl. Elaine would never have spent that kind of money for business clothes. Now I know what Lou is talking about when she said that sometimes her cases required an extensive clothes allowance.*

Elaine got another call and it was Antonio again checking in on her and that he just wanted to say good night. Elaine looked at her watch and realized it was already 10:30 pm. "Well good night to you too. I was just going to bed. I got the information I was expecting so will get up early tomorrow and check the information with Lou. So, until then my friend, I will say good night."

Antonio quickly said before hanging up, "I hope I'm more than just a friend?"

# Chapter 26

The next morning, Elaine heard Lou out in the kitchen. Elaine put on her robe and mentioned to Lou she had a package from Rich that arrived last evening.

Lou asked, "Since you are up Elaine, would you mind making the coffee as you're so much better at it than me? I'll open my package and get the photos of the conference from Sweden in some sort of order."

Elaine answered, "Sure, I'll bring our coffee and the pictures I took locally to the table where we have more room to compare them."

Lou and Elaine put the photos on the table, then checked to see if they recognized any of the men appearing at both conferences. Elaine said, "Darn, some of my photos are not as good as I hoped they'd be."

Lou said, "I think they're great because I've already found two men that match. We can put them together and make a collage of the best ones and if we continue to be lucky, we may find a visible name tag."

Elaine said, "Let me have a look so I can see if I can find any more matches."

Lou said, "I think we have a case. We'll have to share what we have found so far with TIA."

Elaine said, "It just so happens we have a case and permission from TIA to attend the conference as Antonio and Tom's interpreters. I received a box from Bill containing a suit and all the accessories which will surely make me look as well dressed as you."

Lou laughed and said, "See I told you doing what I do has it's perks."

"You can say that again," Elaine said.

"Well Sis, shall we shower, dress and go to the casino for breakfast? Antonio invited us to join them for breakfast last night, are you game?" asked Elaine.

"I'm really looking forward to seeing Tom again. I think we should take the photos with us and see if the guys recognize anyone," Lou smiled.

Elaine said, "That's a great idea and since we are now dealing with this as a case, we can make decisions to do what we feel is necessary to get the job done."

"We'll take the Rover," Elaine said.

Lou said, "I think we should take both cars in case the guys have different ideas of what we should do with the rest of the morning." Lou continued, "Since Diane started this whole thing, we can also tell them about the body found by the highway patrol. We need them to know this is a dangerous top secret conference and that we're going to take all precautions not to let on we ladies are anything more than their interpreters and perhaps eye candy."

Lou added, "Since they're not familiar with what we do and haven't the skills we do, I think we have to make it clear to Antonio and Tom this is not a fun and games pastime for us."

Elaine didn't tell Lou that she had her suspicions that Antonio already knows what their occupations are.

Elaine pulled in close to the front of the casino and Lou beside her. Elaine called Bill to inform him where they were. Elaine asked Bill if they had found any information on Antonio or Tom yet?

Bill said they had come up with very little. They worked as investigators in Europe, not sure for who yet. He said, "We are always contacted by text on disposable phones. Payments for jobs done were made to an offshore bank in the Cayman Islands, which they had set up on their own. We do know they are highly trained and definitely work for the good guys. We feel it is absolutely fine that you work together and it is very lucky that you met. If we come up with anything more concrete, you'll be the first to know."

Antonio was waiting for Elaine at the entrance of the casino and went up and hugged her, then gave her a "where have you been all my life kiss." She kissed him back soundly. He laughed and said, "I'm so glad we don't play games with our relationship, as I told you before, when I like something, I work hard to get it."

Elaine said quietly, "Is that what this is, more a relationship than anything else?"

Antonio looked at her, reached for her hand and held it tight, looking her straight in the eyes he said, "Hell honey, when this conference thing is over and things are back to normal, you'll see what I mean. For right now I would say, (with your permission) you are my girl!"

He guided her to a booth in the café. Elaine asked, "Could this remain our secret until this conference matter is taken care of?"

"Of course!" Antonio answered.

Elaine thought to herself, *Just in case Antonio, if you don't know by now I kinda like being your girl!*

Lou and Tom joined them in the booth and seemed genuinely happy to see each other. "Good news, Antonio. Lou is going to be my interpreter for the seminar. Did you know Lou speaks many languages? It'll be nice to know what everyone is saying and why for a change."

Happily, their waiter was Richard again. He smiled and asked what they would like to drink. They all ordered coffee and asked for menus. Richard, with his towel neatly on his arm, turned and went to his station to prepare our beverages. Lou said, "I love the way Richard serves his customers. When he is on his way back to his station, he checks to see if anyone else wants coffee. If they have carafes on their table, he checks to see if they need to be refilled. Now watch: on his way back he will serve us first and then take care of the other guests. He may be older, but he covers more tables than any other waiter."

Antonio laughed and said, "I would hire him in a minute if I didn't know the casino management. That wouldn't go over too well. We take care of each other when visiting our respective establishments and respect each other enough to keep our hands off each other's hired help. If you are lucky enough to find a good one, you don't want anyone, especially friends to steal them from you."

Richard returned with their meals, refilled their mugs of coffee and served fresh squeezed orange juice. They had been talking for a long time when Elaine looked at her watch and asked Antonio if he wanted to take a ride to the center and check on his invitation and make sure he could bring an interpreter, while she took a quick run.

Lou asked Tom if he wanted to ride with her and he could do the same; however, she had a stop to make and certainly would not be running. Antonio paid the check and they left.

## Chapter 27

Elaine and Antonio walked to the Rover and waited for the car to unlock and got in. It was the first time Antonio rode in the Rover and he liked the way the seat adjusted for his size and weight. It was like it was doing everything but taking his photo. He said that to Elaine.

Elaine laughed and looked to the side for a second and said to Antonio, "How do you know it didn't?"

Antonio laughed.

Elaine explained, "There are many fail safe features in this car, one of them being that just not anyone is allowed to drive it. Of course, you would have to know how to start it and that alone is difficult to do if your photo ID isn't entered in the system. Only persons in the system can use the security equipment. One can't be too careful when out working cases."

Antonio made note of this.

"Where shall we go first, to the center so you register and get your ID tag and hopefully one for me, your personal interpreter? Or you could come with me to run some errands," Elaine asked.

Antonio thought it would be good if she dropped him off at the center while she did her errands. He would meet her at the coffee shop patio in an hour.

Elaine made her way to Ace Hardware. She went through the roundabout and kept right and went all the way to Ace Hardware. She needed some more water; she might possibly check out the whole store. She walked around with the cart picked up the water and proceed to see what might tickle her fancy, such as something to leave for Lou's so-called friend's cottage. Elaine knew it was owned by TIA. *What man did Lou know that called it his cottage? Hum, that sister of mine has "some explaining to do." Just not at this time*, she thought. There was nothing that took her eye, so she went to check out and stood in line.

She got the older Irish lady from before to wait on her. "Sure, an it's water again for you young lady," she said "Might I suggest you check out the sunglasses over there on your way out; they are polarized and full sun protection for sensitive eyes."

Elaine smiled at her and as she paid for the water gave her a "thanks dear."

Elaine went over to the sunglass counter and liked what she saw and purchased three pairs. One for her one for Lou. She paid for them and went to her car. She was sure that she had spent enough time at Ace Hardware for Antonio to be at the coffee shop. She put the water in the boot of the Rover and headed back.

Elaine pulled into the parking lot at the patio area and there was Antonio with a cup of coffee and big smile on his face. He said, "Hi, babe. What do you want and I'll get it for you?"

"Same as you," she replied.

With that he excused himself and went and got Elaine a coffee. Antonio sat the coffee down and bent over and kissed her on the top of her head and said, "What took you so long? It seems I waited for you my whole life."

"Well, you certainly have a way with words," she laughed lightly, with a warm expression on her face.

Antonio said, "There are more words coming when this conference is over and things go back to normal...but until then, nothing is normal around you, is it?"

"While you were at the conference did you hear anything important or did you see anyone you recognized from Sweden? Did you get the name tags, did you hear from Tom?" Elaine asked out of breath.

"My, my, for such a tiny person, you certainly have a lot of questions. Let's not talk business here, but back at the casino. We can go through the photos and see if I recognized any of them while I was walking around and checking the place out. Okay?"

They got in the Rover and this time both doors unlocked and they both got in. "I guess I passed the security check from the last time I rode in this car. Does that mean I can drive this beauty?" Antonio said, as the seat belt fastened around him.

Elaine said, "I'm the only driver until the dashboard lights up and tells me it's okay for you to drive. You are most likely being checked out further, like, are you a good guy or one of the bad guys. That's my expertise, sizing up a person (so to speak) and doing an in-depth profile."

"Tell me more love, have you come to a conclusion where I am concerned or are you playing games?"

Antonio said softly, "What is your conclusion to date?"

Elaine was driving toward the casino and in a sly sexy voice said, "I may have to do more than just talk to get a complete profile. I haven't decided yet.

Antonio laughed and said, "I look forward to that part of the profiling with great anticipation. After this adventure of ours Mrs. North, we must surely find out."

Antonio told Elaine to park in the back near the exit door as he had a key. They both got out and walked arm in arm into the casino. Antonio mentioned that he and Tom both have suites on this floor reserved for executives and dignitaries. It has all the bells and whistles to protect the identity of the people staying here.

They went into the suite and Elaine put the photos on the table. They spread them out and Antonio pulled out an enlarger in order to bring the persons in the photo up close and personal. Antonio was looking slowly and came upon the photo of the security guard and the man he was escorting to his car. "There," he said, "this man was in Sweden as was the security guard. I believe he was on the platform as one of the speakers at the conference."

"This is getting interesting now, Mr. North," Elaine said.

"Yes indeed, Mrs. North. We now have a case of, why, when and what this conference is all about and to think we came upon this accidentally."Antonio continued, "You should contact your employer and tell them if they want Tom and I to pursue this with you they need to let us know. Tell them Tom and I usually go solo, so if we are working with you and your employer, we must all work as a team. No matter what the outcome we must follow all leads and then have a follow-up after each day. If I feel we can discount one part...and your agency another...all facts must be pursued. You have your way of working and we have ours. At the end of the day, we must come to our own conclusions and proceed from there. They can still give you instructions to follow but if I ask you for assistance as though you work for me, will that be okay with them?"

Elaine and Antonio kept checking out the photos and found many more men that were known to have been in Sweden. Elaine said they should Mark the ones Antonio recognized then have Tom and Lou identify the ones they have seen. They would then send the confirmed photos to TIA. "This will prove to be most important especially if they place a priority on what I send," Elaine told Antonio. She didn't tell him the name of her employer, but then there is plenty of time for the employer to do that on their own.

Antonio contacted Tom and asked if he was handy or was he busy. "Lou and I are pulling into the parking lot of the casino now. What can we do for you?" Antonio told Tom about the photos and details over the phone and suggested they meet in the café. "Elaine will give Lou the information and photos for both of you to select the persons you can identify."

Tom said, "Will do, and we'll meet you in the café."

# Chapter 28

They went into the cafe and Lou and Tom were seated at their usual booth. Antonio said that he hoped they got the waiter they had the last few times. "He has a sixth sense when it comes to what you want," he said.

"You mean the waiter, Richard, that you wish you could hire," Elaine said as she poked him in the side.

"That's the one dear," Antonio said, as they sat down in the booth.

Tom looked at them and asked, "Did you have a productive day? Did you take care of business as well as have some fun?"

"What do you think," Antonio said under his breath.

Elaine looked at Lou and she nodded.

Antonio said, "I have a special package to give each of you for the conference. You won't need any other visible objects but the ones in your respective envelopes. Inside you will receive a specially made tablet to take notes, photos, record conversations or send messages to each other. The conference security can't detect your tablets as anything but regular tablets. If you record a conversation and they speak any language but English it will be received as their language. If possible, note the name of the person talking or the number on his/her identification tag. This will prove useful later when trying to identify/track the person speaking. In order for everyone in the group to hear what is being said you will press the code number. Only the four of us know the code. Another thing in the package will be a throw away phone each a different color. The only way to answer or make a call is by face recognition. Let's have breakfast here tomorrow morning. If you have any questions or need demonstrations of the equipment, we can do it at breakfast. Try and remember as many names as possible and faces when meeting the attendees. Also, I want you and Lou to remember not to bring purses or briefcases. Security always opens them and most of the time have a scanner that you don't know about that will do a quick search. They can use a wand that is in their hand or it is imbedded in the table they set the object on. Be sure to have nothing hidden on your body such as weapons. It's better not take chances of being checked in other ways. It would delight these men if they could catch us with something. I can't impress on you enough that they would escort you out and probably to a secure place to search you further. I have seen it done and know the results of their tactics. It's not pretty, trust me."

Elaine piped up, "As much as Lou and I understand you are trying to keep us safe, you need to know we are well versed when it comes to safety. We grew up traveling the world and from the time we were little we knew the different customs of almost every country. Our parents took us all over the world and we had tutors to make sure we knew what to do in the face of danger."

Elaine realized that maybe she sounded like she was scolding Antonio, but then he had to know they were skilled in things beyond the normal person. *I guess he took it in stride because he didn't even raise an eyebrow*, she thought.

They paid the check and got up as Tom said, "We have things to do ladies so if you don't mind, we'll walk you to your cars and meet you back here in the morning."

As they were walking to the car, Antonio grabbed Elaine's hand and held it tight. He bent down and kissed her on the top of her head and whispered, "You are a spitfire beautiful and I admire your style. Never change, okay? I want you to know I'm falling in love with you!"

Elaine smiled and said she had deep feelings for him as well. She was elated to hear that he understood the essence of her and admired her the way she was: a woman of substance. He knew she was smart and could handle herself in any situation. She thought to herself, *How did I get so lucky to find a man that loves me for me and not for what I am supposed to be? Today's world has to change. The life of Mr. & Mrs. North is out of date and doesn't exist anymore.*

Antonio held her close and said, "Goodbye," with a forget-me-not type kiss. "Till tomorrow, love."

Lou started out of the parking lot after she and Tom said their good-byes. Elaine followed her but not too close. They went down the long road past The Purple Pub, which gave Lou chills knowing April was a casualty that should not have happened. She wondered if Diane was censured or moved back to an in-house position where she would have to work her way back to field agent.

# Chapter 29

Lou pulled in the driveway of the cottage first and felt something was not quite the same. She pulled in and stayed in the Sonata. Lou quickly messaged Elaine to proceed with caution.

Elaine heeded the message and parked in the fire station parking lot a few doors down from the cottage where she informed TIA and Lou by message.

Elaine left word she was going to run down the road about three houses and cross the street, which would give her a clear path of vision to see what was going on around the cottage.

She was carrying a few more goodies that were for special occasions like this one. She walked into the clearing at the back of the house next to the cottage as if she lived there. She noticed the back door of their cottage was half open and a light was on. She crept between the garage and Lou's car, slowly opened Lou's car door, and got in. Lou said she didn't see any movement inside, only that the door was open. . . .

The dashboard flashed and an "all clear" signal displayed. The indoor cameras and heat sensors showed no one was in the cottage. TIA said the cleaning crew came and cleaned up the cottage; they also restocked the fridge of everything they might need to last them a week. Once the case at the conference started

Elaine and Lou were not to go anywhere in town unless they were with Antonio and Tom.

Elaine made her way back to the Rover. She pulled it into the cottage driveway and parked beside Lou's car. When she got into the cottage, she saw a package on the kitchen table marked "Lou."

Lou went into her bedroom with her package and shortly came out wearing a designer suit with all the accessories, just like the ones Elaine received earlier in the week. Their outfits were just enough alike that one would easily know that the foursome represented the same company...the invitees and their interpreters.

Special fabric was used for their suits and accessories. There should be no problem with wands or any other detectors. Lou said, "Rich did an excellent job with my clothes, which is a surprise as you know how fussy I am. Well, mark one up for the company."

"We can now say Bill and Rich have good taste," Elaine replied.

"Our dinners are ready for the microwave and the bar has been replenished as well. Now that is what I call a vacation," Lou said with a laugh.

"What do you want to drink while we get the photos ready to send to TIA? Do you have any further information than what we already know about this case?" Lou asked.

"Not really, except we're to keep our eyes open for anyone paying particular attention to Tom and Antonio. They have participated in these types of conferences before and security might be curious as to why they are living in the USA. Both Tom and Antonio are used to working separately, so the advantage of us being their interpreters is that we think as a team. We think alike and we usually don't have to talk to each other to know what the other is thinking."

They had a glass of their favorite wine and a small plate of snacks to go along with it. The photos were compiled and sent to their handlers, Bill and Rich, along with Lou's written comments.

Lou and Elaine were both impressed with the choice of staff TIA had sent to take care of the cottage. In fact, it reminded the twins of Nanny and Uncle Harry. The restocked food items seemed to be all of their favorites. The special touches in the bedroom (fresh flowers and the way the linens on the bed were arranged) was too good to be true. But then they were in California, or were they?

The girls called their handlers to let them know how their day went and that the photos were sent.

Antonio called and said, "With the conference starting at 9:00 a.m. sharp, we should meet at the casino café at 7:00 a.m. to go over what our plan of action will be."

Elaine thought, *This should be an interesting business meeting following Antonio's lead, since we all are used to working on cases solo. It will surely be an adjustment all the way around.*

The day came to a close and it was time for the news and then bed.

The next morning the twins arrived at the casino café with time to spare. Antonio and Tom waved them over to their usual table. They ordered breakfast and then got down to business.

Antonio suggested they try and get as many fingerprints of attendees as possible. "This added with any photo's we take will be a great help in identifying criminals. We mustn't leave any of our prints or DNA on glasses or any surfaces. We can wipe down any surfaces we touch with the special wipes that were in our packages. If there are any agenda changes, we will just go with the flow and see where it leads us and what information we will receive. We'll each work the room by observing and listening.

Hopefully, we will get enough information to find out what really is going on in this conference."

Antonio asked if anyone had any questions. None were asked, so he said, "Okay team, let's get to work and stay safe."

# Chapter 30

Antonio and Tom entered the conference center with their interpreters (Elaine and Lou) close behind. They were checked in and given their ID badges and the schedule of activities, starting with several individual speakers. They got set up and fired up their tablets. When each speaker spoke, they would take a photo and record the speech. Should Tom or Antonio need to listen in on some other conversation close by, one of the twins would leave their tablet facing the speaker and the other twin would maneuver her tablet to face the persons Tom or Antonio were interested in overhearing. Where ever the tablet is pointing, it will immediately hone in on the person/persons one is trying to hear. Noises in between are eliminated, just like some hearing aids that take away background sounds or lessen them.

After each speaker spoke, they had a fifteen minute break. This was the time Lou and Elaine could mingle and maybe be lucky enough to get a fingerprint or two. Tom and Antonio would go to the loo and record conversations, take photos of faces and their badges at the same time while they washed up and dried their hands. Elaine and Lou waited for them to return where they would casually meet them with a bottle of water and napkins to remove their fingerprints when finished. They would all move to sit in another area which exposed them to different guests from other countries and repeat the process over and over again.

Lou and Elaine were amazed how natural it felt working with Tom and Antonio. Hopefully, good things and information will come of it. The ladies did not know if the guys really needed interpreters or not. They would know by tonight. Their being able to take photos and understand what they are saying is a great asset to this case.

When the last speaker is done for the day, guests are invited to discuss with the hosts how they are enjoying the conference and if it's meeting everyone's expectations or if there needs to be more added to the agenda at the next conference.

What has to be done, who, when, and where all this is to take place will be subliminally disclosed at the conference by each speaker. Antonio, Tom, Elaine and Lou along with the help of their recordings, will hopefully come to fully understand these answers.

The foursome decided to have drinks at a local bistro where they enjoyed an hour of conversation and to think about what they'd heard and just relax before they returned to the casino suites and correlate their information and hopefully be able to make some sense of what they'd learned, eliminate the exaggerated words, and try and get down to just the facts. Speakers can really run on and say nothing. It's a trick to know what to eliminate as fluff.

Antonio asked, "Ladies do you want to go home or work in our suites?"

Lou looked at Elaine and their thoughts were the same, as usual. Lou said, while looking into Tom's eyes, "What do you think Tom?"

Lou melted with his quick answer, "Why don't I take Lou to my suite and go over what she and I have found out and sort it all out. I'll call you when we want to get together and formulate our results."

Antonio and Elaine did not need to say a word, but Antonio said smiling, "Makes perfect sense to me."

Elaine drove back to the casino and parked near the back exit. They both got out of the Rover and heard it lock and walked hand in hand to the exit door, where Antonio put his key card into the slot and went in. Out of a habit Antonio checked to make sure the door locked when he shut it. Elaine noticed that as that was what she always did... No reason to take chances leaving it open and endangering everyone on the floor. Elaine thought to herself, *I wonder how many more things we have in common?*

They came to Antonio's suite and entered. Antonio said, "Take a seat at the table let's coordinate everything we saw, said, heard and did while at the conference. Listening to the speakers' words spoken in a subliminal manner would be noticed only by those knowing there's a message beyond the surface." Antonio then asked Elaine, "Please jot down any word or phrase that seems to come up frequently with the different speakers. I'll do the same. I know you were possibly not paying attention to what the speaker was saying but listening to the content."

*Au contraire,* Elaine thought. *As a criminal interpreter and criminal psychologist that's my expertise. Sometimes it's how they speak, their mannerisms, what they are leaving out and words they exaggerate or pause after saying, is important and you should pay the most attention to it. They may sound somewhat different than the usual speaker's tone of voice and the true meaning comes through.*

Antonio had his list and suggested they see what hidden message all the speakers were trying to get across to the real controllers involved in some overt plot involving or might involve the countries they represented.

So, once again it seems they are both on track when it comes to back road intrigue. Elaine handed a list to Antonio and she said, "Let's check off the words or phrases we both heard. You jot them down and then we can see what we come up with. It may be a country, person, etc."

Antonio said, "I see you are on top of your game. We have several duplicate words; now we must come up with their hidden meaning."

Elaine said, "Let's start with the words we both selected and then the ones we noticed by ourselves. We both have Germany, Turkey, China, Syria, Iran, Taiwan, and England. As I see it, any one of these might be of importance to the message itself. Now to the question: is it one person involved or the country itself? If a name of a person comes up, let's try and figure out what country he represents or if we think he is involved in the plot itself.

Antonio said, "We both indicated Taiwan. What do we know about what is happening over there?"

Elaine said, "I understand a Taiwanese chip giant, is building a hedge against China. They go under the name of TSMC, or Taiwanese Semiconductor Manufacturing Company, which is the biggest maker of leading-edge chips. TSMC outlined a $40 billion plan to expand and upgrade a United States production hub that is currently building in Phoenix and are under contract to build two plants there. The projection is to produce the product called three-nanometer chips. Eventually, the new plan would upgrade to four-nanometer technology. It should start production as soon as 2024. I know they have already broken ground."

*I would enjoy this guessing game*, Elaine thought, *if only it didn't have clandestine meanings. I hope Lou remembers some of what went on at the conference in Sweden. She's good at plots and her recall of events, as well as people...you will find out she is uncanny.*

"We've connected China and Taiwan, now where does Syria, Iran, Germany and England come into this scenario?" Elaine suggested they go for a walk on the beach to clear their minds, "What say you?"

Antonio answered, "That's a good idea. We can make reservations for dinner at the café if you want on our way out." Elaine hesitated and said, "As much as I would love to, Lou and I should go to the cottage and check for messages."

"It was just a thought, dear, as I would like to enjoy your company a little longer today."

Elaine said softly, "We must keep our eyes on the whole doughnut and not the hole in it."

Antonio laughed and said, "Girl, who in the world gave you so many old-fashioned expressions?"

Elaine said, "My Nanny did!"

Laughingly he shook his head and said, "I must say, you keep a guy on his toes if not for your looks, intelligence, then the sayings from your youth."

They put on their warm clothes and headed for the beach. They watched the tide wash away some of the sand and bring it back with more rocks showing.

Antonio found a rock that in a half-assed way looked like a heart. He said in all seriousness, "Now this heart is a sign of my love. It may look funny but then, so do I. Nothing in life is perfect, with the exception of you."

Elaine stopped dead in her tracks and laughed out loud saying, "Dear heart, I'm as far from being perfect than anyone else in the world."

They turned around after Antonio realized they'd been walking for an hour or so. He thought to himself, *I can't remember the last time I went walking on the beach for no reason at all but just to clear my mind. Today I walked and didn't think of business, but just the two of us. A wonderful feeling, just wonderful.*

They went to the back of the casino and entered through the door and again Antonio put his hand on the doorknob and checked to see if it was locked. They went to the door of the suite and Antonio heard the phone ring.

Tom said, "Where have you been, I've called several times? I hope I didn't call at a bad time?"

Antonio laughed and said, "No such luck! We went for a walk on the beach. What's up Tom?"

"Well, we've matched everything we could and coordinated the results now we want to compare our findings with yours so we're ready for tomorrow. Oh also, Lou says she has to go home and won't be able to eat with us."

"Funny," Antonio said, "same here. I sometimes forget we're with two businesswomen and not just dates. Come over, I'll unlock the door for you and Lou to come in."

When Lou arrived, Elaine asked her if she heard from anyone from TIA.

Lou said she hadn't heard anything and she has a lot of information she needs from Rich.

Elaine mentioned she needed more information from Bill as well. Elaine said, "Guess we have to light a fire under these guys to make sure we receive it by tonight so we can be prepared for 'what tomorrow brings.'"

# Chapter 31

The ladies decided to leave while it was still light out. Antonio said, "Tom and I will go over all of our findings and combine them. He continued directing his conversation to Tom and Lou, "Elaine and I have come up with some important facts...adding your findings, we just might be able to pinpoint exactly what to concentrate on tomorrow during the last day of the conference."

Lou and Elaine were escorted to their cars, where they said their goodbyes. Antonio said, "Let's do a conference call later tonight. Once we have coordinated all of our information, we can send Bill and Rich our findings. We can meet at the café for breakfast tomorrow and go over our final business notes. Hopefully, your handlers will have information of interest to pass on to us that will lead us to the mission these countries are working on or where they think the next conference will be held...and...there will be another!"

Elaine said calmly, "It'll be taken care of and any necessary suggestions and/or instructions they give us we'll all talk it over. Just know that all four of us must pay strict attention to details that may deviate this final conference day. The agenda could be the answer to some things we haven't connected. Even which speaker may or may not be scheduled. Oh, also be alert to those who come tomorrow in case they were not present yesterday. We need to know all the faces in attendance."

Tom said to Antonio, "It's been some time since we worked on cloak and dagger stuff which most certainly is going on here. We need to find out if it directly involves the United States or just indirectly."

Antonio replied, "With America in the state it's in at the moment one might read more into it than meets the eye. Oh, my gosh. Elaine has me saying these old sayings now too."

Tom laughed and said, "Lou comes up with some doozies too. From what I understand, it has to do with their Nanny that raised them. Nanny Brown sounds like quite a lady and she is one of the top agents TIA has."

Elaine and Lou arrived safely to the cottage and entered the warm cozy great room. Lou said, "Let's go over all of our combined information. I'll make a breakdown of what exactly we are looking for with the following headings:

1. Coordinate all four of our lists.
2. List all countries we know were at the conference.
3. Separate allies from problem countries.
4. Check all photos, badge numbers, names, countries/companies they represent.
5. Phrases or words that were repeated by all speakers.
6. Where the next conference could/will take place.

Once this is done, we can send the information to the powers that be, and hope at least one of them will get the job done and forward the information to Antonio and Tom."

Lou handed Elaine her list and they proceeded with the list and separated all the paperwork, photos, and miscellaneous information acquired that hadn't been connected to anything as yet. "Shall we start?" Elaine said.

Elaine continued, "Countries that have hosted the conference are Sweden and the United States. We have found attendees that we must view as dangerous to our country. These countries are up to something overt which could cause great strife if we don't come up with what they are up to soon."

Lou held up her list and checked off consistencies with Elaine's list. Lou said, "We have China, Iran, Syria, Turkey—the troubled countries, and Germany, Taiwan, and England (allied countries) which are a total of seven countries to keep an eye on. We can't exclude any country at this point in time, allied or not."

Elaine said, "The United States-China relationship is the most complex bilateral relationship for the U.S. They have found common ground on issues of trade, investment, and security. Key issues remain unresolved, and the potential for divergence is real as China becomes an economic powerhouse, a military force in Asia, and a potential rival to U.S. hegemony (domination, social, cultural, ideological, or economic influence exerted by a dominant group). China is also purchasing everything they can get their hands on throughout the United States including but not solely, farmland, fresh water, lakes with surrounding land, prime property, manufacturing plants, and coastline property. Also land near military bases. Then we have the Islamic Republic of Iran and the United States have had no formal diplomatic relationship since the Iranian takeover of the American embassy on November 4, 1979. Iran with their nuclear operations that have never completely shut down to my satisfaction. World problems caused by Syria. Syria advocates Arab Socialism and Arab Nationalism with their motto being 'unity, freedom, socialism.' Relations between Syria and the United States are currently nonexistent. We know that Turkey is a key NATO ally and critical regional partner, and the United States is committed to improving the relationship between the two countries. This relationship is trying as Turkey sometimes waffles between what is right or wrong. If Antonio and Tom come up with these same conclusions as to problem countries that attended the conference, TIA must be notified immediately and not wait for something untoward to happen. The international agency (TIA) is obligated to keep ahead of everyone else when it comes to knowing what is going on in the underground black ops."

Lou said, "We know the possible problem countries, which is no surprise to anyone, so let's examine these coincidences. I think we should call TIA and tell them they are causing problems. If they don't know anything, for heaven's sake tell us. We'll have to go rogue and try and secure something from our end. This is something that should never be our responsibility as we don't have the equipment nor the ability to double check the information we come up with. One thing I know for sure is that the more we find out, the more dangerous circumstances will be. The truth is what we need and now! Bill and Rich must get their part done for us to continue."

Elaine said, "Let's call Antonio and Tom and see if they have come up with anything we can talk over tonight. We can't wait until tomorrow for TIA and we know Antonio has contacts all over the world. Maybe they can shed some light on what is going on."

Antonio answered the conference call on the second ring, "Hello, beautiful ladies. What can I do for you?"

Elaine explained about the four countries that could be at the conference for more than what the agenda states. "Reading between the lines we have come up with who we think are the possible countries representing the dangerous underground, working against us and the security of the world...in the long run."

Antonio said, "Tom and I came up with four problem countries as well: China, Iran, Syria and Turkey."

"Well," Elaine said, "we did the same and we haven't closed in on what they're planning to do. There are so many nefarious things these countries could plan. We also listed our allies, Germany, Taiwan, and England to keep an eye on."

Lou added, "We do know something's up and it's not for the betterment of the world. We also know there will be one more conference to solidify their intent. We can't wait for them to initiate their plans, so we must ascertain what they are going to do before it's too late. What have you and Tom come up with other then the four countries holding the strings?"

Antonio spoke, "We have sent out feelers to our backroad pack and hope to hear soon. That's all we can say right now. No luck on your end from your handlers I guess?"

Not wanting to complain about their end of this situation Elaine said, "We're hoping to hear anytime now. Antonio, with your knowledge of overt operations along this line of business, we were thinking maybe you and Tom had some suggestions as to what we should be doing on our side instead of waiting... I guess waiting is not one of my fortes?"

"One thing we have decided for sure is that if there are new persons attending the last day, we should try and capture their photo, badge number, and find out their country of origin," Antonio said.

Tom said, "Elaine, you and Lou should use your skills to introduce yourselves to those we feel are important, especially those from the four countries we previously mentioned. That will shorten our having to check all those that enter. When you spot the persons of interest or anyone speaking their language, send a message to us. They could possibly send only one person from that country in the effort not to be too obvious as having not attended the prior days."

Elaine agreed, "That's a good idea. Lou and I will walk the room listening for persons and/or person speaking their languages. I know Lou and I will both be doing a profile of those we feel are of interest. If there's a group representing one of the 'nefarious four,' we will select the weakest link for extraction and questioning."

Antonio said, "We need to select someone that won't be missed by the rest of the group. He/she must be one that we feel would talk or at least discuss and disclose much needed information. If we are lucky enough to find this person early enough, we could trick him/her into going into an area where he/she can be removed from the conference unobserved and taken to a safe house for interrogation. If that person is with a group, we could leave a message with the conference receptionist to forward to the group that he/she will not join them until later in the evening. If this person is alone, no one will know until it is too late."

Elaine said, "We must go to extreme measures to obtain anything that'll help us get on top of what is going on. We need to make sure we're on the right track and obtain some firm sources to check on between now and the next conference."

Lou said, "I think the future conference will be held in a year. I recall overhearing one of the countries talking about it. 'Next year will be the icing on the cake.' I wasn't worried about that country as it was one of our allies. However, now that things are connecting and the puzzle is clearer, I now believe it's very significant."

Elaine said, "Those are the little things we are listening for. Lou you may just have come up with one of our missing links."

Antonio said, "I contacted TIA while we were talking and they just sent me a fax stating they'll arrange for the 'all necessary takeaway' if we find the right person. They said they would have the extraction team ready one way or the other."

Elaine said, "I believe Lou has great recall and her ability to remember 'a year from now' is very valuable information. Narrowing down the time is most important."

Tom said, "I didn't make much of it at the time; however, I recall the second speaker saying something about Ocean Shores reminds him of this time of year in London. Could that mean it will be held in London next year?"

Antonio suggested, "By knowing London and next year (if we find a person to interrogate) we can act as if we already know where the conference will be held and that it's next year. Hopefully, that person will tell us the month and day and what else we're looking for. Do you ladies know just how much has been cleared up by this phone conversation? We have possibly eliminated two of the most important facts, location, and date. Let's all get some rest as 6:00 a.m. comes fast. I have arranged for the café to expect us. Good night, see you tomorrow!"

Elaine said, "We'll contact our handlers to the possible place and year. Night and sweet dreams."

Lou said after they hung up, "Elaine, our ETA tomorrow at the casino is 6:00 am. So let's make one last check to see if TIA left a package for us. I sure hope Bill or Rich helped us out. Better late than never."

Lou went to the back porch and checked the BBQ. There were two packages, one for Elaine and one for herself. Lou said, "There's a package for each of us this time. I'm going to check mine out before I go to bed. I'll never sleep for wondering what Rich has found out. I've almost forgotten all the things I needed to have him find out for me."

"Same here!" Elaine said, picking up her package.

At the top of the page Bill wrote to Elaine, "There'll be agent's undercover around the conference hall in case you need them along with an extraction team. Also, watch what you ask around the person of interest, we don't want the other men in the group to get wise to how vulnerable this guy may be. If anyone in the group is wise to your ability to profile and you're not just another pretty face and a smart woman at that, they will watch him like a hawk or double up around him which means he can't leave before the end of the day. My suggestion is that if you do find out anything or suspect he might be the one to takeaway, smile and excuse yourself and start talking to other men. Look like you are interested in all the men and not just one man. They would like to think you are on the prowl and not intelligent enough to be an agent."

*Thanks Bill*, Elaine thought. *I don't think I have to be told how to profile all of the men at once and not notice if one or more are checking me out. For heaven's sake, in our line of work we learn that in grade school.*

Lou looked over her package and laughed at some of the things Rich said. Lou said, "I know he's making sure I'm safe, but this is not my first rodeo."

Elaine replied, "That's what Bill intoned to me. However, it's good we know that TIA agents are undercover and able to remove/takeaway the man they need to get more facts from."

In Elaine's package, one of the things she had asked Bill was information about Antonio. She thought: *He found out exactly what I already knew. He's a two person operation who covers all the backroad work in Europe, etc. No prints on file, gets paid offshore, which in turn he sends to unknown banks, and not traceable. Very reliable and recently retired. He has a friend/colleague who assists him with anything he needs...he has contacts that no one knows who they are or where they are.*

On the typed note Bill wrote, "I tell you, Elaine, with him on your side, if indeed that's who he is, you have nothing to worry about. At least that's what 'the powers that be' feel. My guys are pissed that they couldn't connect all the dots. It took them this long because essentially, Antonio is a 'ghost.'"

Lou got up and said, "I'm taking a shower and then off to bed. Good night, Sis."

# Chapter 32

Elaine got up the next morning and made coffee. She poured a cup and took it into Lou where she was gathering up her paperwork and placing it in her attaché case. "Thanks for the coffee!" Lou said. "I know we can't take our attaché cases with us into the center but we may need something out of it at breakfast."

Elaine said a short time later, "All ready to leave, Lou. You should probably warm up your Sonata as it was pretty chilly overnight."

"Thanks. I didn't think of that. I can also say I will not miss this cold weather. I guess you can call me a 'California woman.'" Lou added, "You know, Elaine. I closed the case I was working on, so after today I hope we can say this case here in Ocean Shores is closed also."

Elaine mentioned, "'The powers that be consider my one case closed, although I'm not so sure, but then they're my boss. I can say, once we finalize the extraction at this conference we should be finished here in Ocean Shores. As for the conference as a whole, we may find ourselves semi-closing it until next year in London."

*Lou came out looking like a million bucks in her form-fitting designer suit that would keep everyone thinking about anything but the conference,* thought Elaine.

Elaine said, "Let's head out for the casino, Lou. I'll see you at the café."

As always, Elaine left first and arrived at the casino. She found two parking spots together nearest the front door. She notified TIA that they should watch both cars until after the conference. Tom would be driving them today.

Lou pulled up beside Elaine and they walked into the casino together where they went directly to the café. Richard was waiting for them and escorted them to their usual booth. With his towel over his arm and a smile he asked, "What can I do for my ladies today...the usual?"

"For sure," Lou said.

Elaine sat on one side and Lou on the other. Lou said, "I hope Tom and Antonio don't keep us waiting even though we're a little early. I can't wait to hear what they've come up with."

Looking up, Lou saw them coming and told Elaine. Elaine blushed, as she turned her head to see her man sit down. He gave her a big hug and squeezed her hand. Tom sat down by Lou and mentioned how lovely she looked today and it's a shame they have to waste their time on this conference.

"I know," Lou said.

"Tell you what, Lou, how about you park your car at the cottage and I'll fly you back to California?" Tom asked.

Antonio said looking at Elaine, "You know what honey, let's take the long way home to Malibu in your Rover. We can enjoy the sights."

"Lou and I'll talk and let you know after the conference. We have to close our part of this case before we can finish our vacation."

Tom said, "The Fourth of July festivities aren't looking too good. The recent forecast is for heavy fog, overcast and a possibility of rain. We'd be lucky to see any fireworks."

Lou replied, "Well, we'll have to try and arrange something on our own."

Tom whispered in her ear and said, "Like fireworks of our own?"

*Lou gave him that magical smile of hers and I assume whatever he said to her was to her liking,* Elaine thought.

Antonio said to everyone, "We know that TIA has arranged for agents to be around the conference hall if we need them, which with luck we will...thanks to Lou and Elaine. The first thing for us to do is check the attendance list for any new attendees. We'll send the new names/countries to TIA to investigate."

Richard brought out their food and refilled their coffee cups. They ate their food and enjoyed a few moments of social conversation before leaving for the conference.

Antonio said, "Tom will drive us to the coffee house where there will be a limousine waiting to drive us to the conference center. We'll be arriving early, but I'm sure we'll be allowed in as staff will most likely assume we are VIP's considering our arrival in a limo. I've instructed the driver to be outside the door and waiting for us to leave at the end of the day. He'll take the long way back to the coffee house to make sure we haven't been followed. We'll get into Tom's car and go back to the casino and have room service. Once in the suite we can check and list everything we saw, where everyone gathered and list the ones we noticed acted differently. I'm sure Tom and I will appear to have weak kidney's considering how often we go to the loo. We sometimes have great luck and find out lots of things while washing our hands, etc."

Elaine said, "Lou and I have routines we follow. We walk around as casual as possible but at the same time smiling and nodding at many people."

Lou said, "The men usually think they know me and or wonder which of them I knew. It keeps them on their toes."

Elaine added, "At the same time we check their language and name tags. One of us will stand close to the receptionist as she checks off the names of attendees. We've found on other cases we were working on together, that the attendee's name that they don't check off are usually well known by the staff and sometimes are the ones pulling the strings in these types of meetings or conferences."

"I think we have gone over everything we can," Antonio said. They got up from the table, paid the check, and headed for Tom's car. The girls sat in the back and fussed with their lipstick and hair.

Tom parked his car out of sight at the coffee house and as instructed the limousine pulled up beside them and picked them up. They drove around the block and then up to the conference center entrance. The driver opened the doors and helped the ladies out of the limousine—then the men. He tipped his hat and said he would return when the conference was over. "I'll be waiting at the entrance for you."

Antonio said smiling, "Thank you, Paul," and they walked into the conference hall.

Just as Antonio said would happen, the conference personnel looked at their name tag, checked them off the list, and let them enter early. They handed them the agenda for the day and a list of the speakers, etc. With that out of the way, the guys went directly into the washroom and Lou and Elaine moved around the conference room. They took photos of the early birds and workers.

Lou and Elaine stopped near a group of men and listened to hear what language they were speaking. It was apparent as they spoke Mandarin that they were from somewhere in China. Lou was knowledgeable and jotted down some remarks she overheard that might come in handy later. It appeared to anyone that might be watching that the ladies were simply checking their tablets.

Lou and Elaine stopped by a refreshment table and got a cup of coffee and then proceeded to laugh at nothing looking as if they saw something funny and kept walking past that group. The next man standing alone Lou nodded as if she knew him. She kept walking but innocently dropped her pen. The man Lou had nodded to picked it up and said in good English, (possibly from Europe), "I believe you dropped this and might need it."

Lou expressed her thanks and smiled asking, "Where are you from in England?"

He said, "London. How did you know?"

She said, "It's on your name tag!" Then she laughed and thanked him again, but not before taking another photo...now she had his front and back. She continued on to where Elaine had stopped.

Lou said, "We have two down. One from London and the group from China." They moved closer to the entrance and Lou said softly to Elaine, "Do you hear what I hear, someone speaking Bulgarian." Lou got close enough and read his name tag. It said he was from Turkey. *He must be a Turkified Pomak.*

Elaine said, "Let's try our list of people that are expected today, the one Antonio sent us. It should be on our tablet."

Lou continued, "Now, we're really on a roll. Let's keep mingling."

"Sounds good to me," Elaine said while continuing to walk towards more attendees.

Lou said, "I see Antonio and Tom looking our way. Shall we walk over to them and add anything to our lists that they might have noticed or found out?" Lou went over to Tom and talked to him, while Elaine moved towards Antonio.

Antonio asked her where they should sit when the speakers started. He asked her to check out when they would be allowed to enter the conference room. Elaine walked over to three men standing close to the conference room. As she got closer, she heard them speaking in French. She asked in English if they knew how long they thought it might be before they would allow people to enter the conference room? One of the men answered her in English and said, "In about 10 minutes."

Elaine thanked him and went back to Antonio.

Lou was watching two people chatting and realized one was Chinese and the other was the Englishman she had asked where in England he was from. *Funny*, she thought, *the Chinese man approached the Englishman and gave him a half hug with his left hand on the Englishman's neck and then shook his hand. Now that is what I call strange, especially for a man from China. The Chinese are usually more formal when greeting a person.*

Lou followed him to the entrance to the conference room at the same time touching Tom's arm and suggested they sit behind the Englishman if at all possible. Something strange just happened and I want to observe him without his knowledge. Tom escorted her and without saying anything, sat her right behind him. Tom spoke softly, "Is this, okay?"

Lou said, "More than okay, I just found our takeaway man."

Tom let Antonio know who they targeted for extraction and why.

Without question, Antonio said, "All will be taken care of. I'll notify the extraction team through TIA. It'll be up to them to handle things from their end. Don't worry. They know what they're doing."

Elaine said to Antonio, "This makes perfect sense now, being that the conference next year may possibly held in London."

Lou and Tom came over and joined Antonio and Elaine.

Tom said, "So far, we have learned someone from London has arrived, a group from Turkey, and a group from China. The one from London is a takeaway."

Elaine said, "Good, we'll check further and during the break the one I feel is another possibility of a takeaway will be the man that spoke Bulgarian and is from Turkey."

Antonio notified TIA. He received notification on his phone from the extraction team that it would be done: *Also, you don't have to tell us where he is. We are on it.*

Elaine and Lou hoped they could spot a representative from Iran...that would be a great profile for them to check out. The girls read each other's mind and smiled. *I wonder if a person from Iran is here undercover? Do the men always wear the traditional men's garment the Shalvar, and Jameh combination, often with a wide belt called Kamarband? Do the women always wear a hijab (scarf), knee length Roo-poosh (coat) and a long dress or pair of pants?*

Elaine queried to Antonio, "Do the Iranians ever wear suits and ties or are they always in their countries traditional attire?"

Antonio replied, "I would imagine they do, but I know for a fact that the men have an anti-necktie sentiment which stems from the 1979 revolution, when the accessory was denounced as a symbol of western cultural oppression."

Antonio asked Lou, "What made you choose the Englishman as the takeaway?"

Lou said, "It was something I observed. I'll tell you later. I can say it also involved a man from China. Extracting the man from China is a no-no because they have a way of answering a question with a smile on their face but mean the opposite. They can't be taken on their appearance or word. If they do that to your face, you won't be able to get them to discuss their intentions in an interrogation situation."

Antonio excused himself and went over to a waiter and spoke to him briefly. He came back and said, "We should leave now before the extraction happens. I'll text Paul to bring the car around." The four of them went to the front door and there was Paul.

"Let's go!" Tom said.

Paul got out of the limousine and opened the doors for the ladies and helped them in. He then opened the opposite doors and Antonio and Tom got in. Paul drove down a few blocks past the turnoff to the coffee house, all the while checking to see if they were being followed. When he was sure it was safe, he drove down a back alley and entered the coffee house parking lot. Paul asked Antonio, "Is there anything further you need, sir?"

Antonio said, "Paul, your service was exemplary. My company will take good care of you. If we are ever in Ocean Shores again, we most certainly will ask for you."

Paul let the passengers out and said, "Thank you, sir!" and drove away.

# Chapter 33

Tom drove all of them to the back of the casino where they all went up to Antonio's suite to have a bite and go over everything they collected during the conference. "First of all," Lou said, "we must notify 'the powers that be' to handle the Englishman with kid gloves. He has a fake mole near his hairline. I saw the man from China put his hand on the back of the Englishman's neck. You can look at the photos of him before and after he went into the conference room. The first photo I took was early in the morning. Tom and I sat behind him and I took a photo of the Englishman and it showed what the man from China had placed on his hairline. I suspect it to be some sort of electronic device filled with information and/or secrets. The extraction team must take him to have it removed so we can decode it and hopefully secure much needed information. So, if you'll excuse me, I need to call TIA immediately."

Elaine did the same. The ladies sent everything they found out so the office could assimilate their own conclusions, as well as find out what was on the mole.

Room service delivered their food and everyone sat down and enjoyed the meal. "Now we can coordinate our next move," Antonio said. "But first, what did they say when you called your people?" Antonio asked Elaine and Lou.

Lou said, "They told me it was okay to go on with my vacation as I wished. I told them I was going to travel back with Tom. My part in this case is finished for now until the next conference. I'll leave my car in the garage where someone will pick it up later. Tom's going to pick me up tomorrow morning and we'll proceed to his place. We'll also check out the restaurant and make sure it will be run properly per your instructions, Antonio."

Elaine said, "I'm not sure what my plans are at this moment; however, Antonio will stay with me and as soon as we receive more information...Antonio and I will take it from there."

Antonio said, "Now that we know what we will do tomorrow, let's get back to finishing all our facts. Lou, you make a list on your tablet of what we think should be checked out as we go forward. Maybe not today, but in the near future. Title it: 'Final Conference.' Use PowerPoint and keep it brief please."

*Final Conference*

1. *Confirm date of conference and location.*

2. *Inform our associates to notify any and all information they hear as soon as they hear it that might involve the future conference. i.e.: countries, agents, undercurrents/unrest in certain areas, no matter how trivial.*

3.  *Was there anything we should know of what was found on the mole. Put there without the knowledge of the Englishman and who on the other end might have been waiting for it.*

4.  *What was the reason for the man from Turkey to be at the conference. A hit man, or what.*

5.  *Check photos of the men from Iran and see if we can find out their names and affiliations.*

"Now Lou, would you please make a separate list for countries that might be pulling the strings on the overt mission they are planning disguised as a conference. Title it: 'String-pullers.'"

*String-pullers*

1.  *China (Purchasing property, waiting for the farmers to be in such bad shape that they will sell to them. Coastline for future shipping ports, allowing Chinese to enter America without being checked, bringing in airborne diseases and pests, labs that are researching their work in secret and the list goes on).*

*2. Iran (They fund Hasbulla and anyone else that will help Muslims fight against USA and Israel.)*

*3. Syria (They are anti-American, want to be a dictatorship...autonomy)*

*4. Russia (Not on our list, but must be considered because of their actions throughout the world, especially against the USA) ...Russia receives arms from most of the countries listed here. Young Russian men coming across our borders, why!!! These men using the excuse they didn't want to fight against Ukraine makes us believe many could be affiliated with the KGB.*

*Allies we should alert:*

*1. England, Germany and Taiwan. (They are our allies and have probably heard of the conference).*

Lou suggested that she and Elaine should probably head back to the cottage. We've a lot of information we need to forward to TIA and information we are expecting.

"Well, ladies, we have a number of things that must be handled as well. Tom and I will follow-up on some things we have to put into motion regarding the conference. We'll notify our contacts and put feelers out on the backroads. We'll walk you ladies down to your cars."

They arrived at their cars and said their goodbyes. Antonio and Elaine shared a long deep kiss.

Surprise, surprise, Lou and Tom did the same. Elaine said softly to Antonio looking at Lou and Tom, "I think something is going on in the car next to mine, don't you?"

"I think you could be right my dear," Antonio chuckled. "I'll call you later, Elaine. Until tomorrow my love," as he backed up out of the way of her Rover.

They exited the casino parking lot as usual and down the road to the cottage. They arrived at the cottage without a hitch. They parked side by side in the back near the garage. The motion lights came on and Elaine opened the back door. They both walked in and were glad to be home. Lou went into the kitchen and put on a pot of water for tea. Elaine put out the tea pot and cups on the kitchen table along with munchies. She put her tablet in front of her and wrote down what she wanted to talk to Bill about, then she went to the back porch and checked for packages. There were two, one for both of them.

Elaine thought, *For once maybe we'll get the information we need and/or they will tell us to come home or take time off for our vacation.* She handed Lou her package. They both filled their cup with tea and opened their packages up.

Lou said, "I'll go into the tv room and call Rich to take care of my case...after I finish this cup of tea." Lou will remind Rich is to make sure that he makes arrangements for Diane Lane to have a talk with her as she has some questions that need to be answered.

Elaine said, "I'll stay at the kitchen table and call Bill. Let's hope we can head back to Malibu or whatever."

"From your mouth to god's ears, Sis," Lou said.

Elaine called Bill who said, "Come on! Come on!"

She answered, "Not on the road, good buddy, here at the cottage."

Bill laughed at Elaine's response.

Elaine continued, "TIA said I could continue my vacation with Antonio. We have decided to return via the Rover. Also, you consider the case of the missing student closed, but I still have a gut feeling something more is going on. Are you sure the agents trailing them are staying close and rotating their surveillance? Because the driver of the RV is sharp...tell them if the RV deviates from the itinerary they gave us to be sure to double up or whatever you feel is necessary to keep them in close, yet not where they'll know they're being watched."

Bill said, "Will do! If you're driving back with Antonio, you have permission to let him know what your gut feeling is. I'll have my agents check further into the parents of Carol. Also, have them check if there is any connection, no matter how little with the conference attendee list. I won't let anything slip through the cracks, Elaine. Just enjoy the rest of your trip back to Malibu. Take your time and stay safe. Over and out!"

Meanwhile, Lou called Rich. Rich said, "Everything pertaining to the Diane Lane case is coming to a close. We were very happy with your initial insight to notify the sheriff to keep the body's identification as 'unknown.' We did the same and nothing was released to the public other than it was a woman. Diane Lane is here at TIA and now fully realizes that her lack of communication with us resulted in the death of April, a poor unsuspecting friend she stayed with. She knows she should have told April the reason she needed a place to stay was that she was being followed. Now Diane will suffer the consequences for her actions. However, Diane has a lot of information she is checking on and using her photos of the conference in Sweden along with the photos that you sent back to TIA. Already she has found the two men that were following her in Ocean Shores...in one of her photos and they were with three other men. So Diane is also helping with the findings referring to the upcoming conference. Your observations at the conference were stellar. With your recordings and photos, these will allow us to follow through with what action we have to take between now and the final conference, as well as verify the location and date. Now you can take your vacation with Tom and relax. With your cases over, you're now on 'downtime.' TIA will contact you when you return to Malibu. If you need anything contact me."

Lou said, "You could do me a favor since Diane is safe. Could you release April's name and give her a proper wake at The Purple Pub where she worked? I think TIA owes her that much."

Rich said, "Consider it done. I'll personally see to it. You're always considerate and appropriate when it comes to what should be done in these types of circumstances. Thanks, Lou!"

# Chapter 34

Lou and Elaine finished their calls and decided to just relax for the rest of the day. Elaine asked, "Have you decided what you are going to do for the rest of your vacation? Go with Tom or do you want to return via the Rover? Antonio will be going back with me and you're welcome to join us."

Lou looked at Elaine with a dreamy smile on her face and Elaine said, "I thought so...so Tom it is! Seems like you have more romance in mind than driving with us!"

They both laughed and thought together, *Finally, what I call a vacation. . . .*

Lou called Tom and they arranged for him to pick her up in the morning where they would fly to Hoquiam. Tom said, "We can stay at my place for a few days or until you get bored and then fly to Malibu. I have to check things at the restaurant to make sure things run smoothly if Antonio and I want to go to California. Hope you don't mind?"

"It sounds wonderful, Tom. We check out the town by car this time and watch the sun rise and set at your place. Is that what you had in mind?" Lou remarked.

"There is nothing I would like better, Lou," Tom said with a smile in his voice.

Antonio called Elaine and they discussed the day and their findings. Elaine reiterated that he should make sure the mole on the Englishman be replaced after being reproduced for further investigation. I don't think he even knows it is on his hairline. Find out what his ETA is for London and have him followed to see if the Chinese are meeting him when he arrives. Also, if no one meets him then he must be followed wherever he goes, as the contact man might be a spy in London. Maybe we could add a detector or some gadget that you are aware of that would keep us informed. I will call my office and check also."

Antonio said, "I had the same thoughts as you, Elaine. I had it taken care of while he was still in custody. He never knew the mole was placed on him. When we interrogated him, we removed it without his knowledge, and replaced it with something undetectable to anyone but us. He thought he was just giving us information that went on in the conference. We gave him some of our information and asked him for clarification. We told him we knew the next conference was to be held next year but didn't get any more details than that. He is very eager to assist us and told us he would confirm the exact place and date the conference will be in London. We found out he's one of ours, albeit a very green agent. When we were finished with him, we told him we'd let everyone in his office know how much we enjoyed our chat with him and let them know he certainly is an asset to their office. So, our case Mrs. North, is over. At least for a year."

Elaine said that after Tom picks up Lou she would drive to the casino and pick him up.

Antonio said, "You know what I think honey? Let's have one last breakfast at the cafe before we leave, just the two of us. Pull in the back parking lot where I will be waiting for you. We can put my things in your car. You can secure the Rover and let them know I will be traveling with you."

Elaine laughed and said, "Oh, silly, I'm way ahead of you. I already told TIA you would be accompanying me and they gave the okay."

"I can't wait for tomorrow and knowing we can take our time going back. If you don't mind, I'd like to go home by way of Hoquiam and check out the restaurant. Tom and Lou might still be there and we can all have dinner together and enjoy dancing and all the things we missed the last time you were there. We can stay at my place, walk on the beach and see the town, does that sound okay?"

Elaine said, "Sounds great. I also want to double check with the police and make sure the case of the murdered woman on the beach is closed."

Antonio said, "Okay. However, sweetness, no more cases! Just vacation and enjoying each other's company without business interfering."

"That's a deal," Elaine replied. "I'll call you in the morning and let you know I am on my way."

Antonio said, "Honey, I need lots of kisses in the morning when you arrive because I didn't receive enough when you left earlier."

Lou said to Elaine, "This vacation is so different from any I have ever had. At first it was so-so. I thought it was going to be boring compared to what I'm used to. I knew you had a case you had to handle and then when we went to Hoquiam and you had that really bad case fall into your lap, believe me I was really wondering what in heavens was happening. I'd normally have a good time being waited on, pampered and doing some shopping...then when you came home and said we were going to dinner at a new restaurant, I was sure it was going to be a mom-and-pop establishment. Then to my complete surprise, that's when our vacation really started. It was so odd to find an upscale restaurant...not to mention meeting Tom and Antonio in that small town."

Elaine and Lou looked at each other and as twins do, thought to themselves, "You can say that again."

Just think we both are going on an adventure we have never been on before—at least me," Elaine said. "You know how I am when it comes to men: I can take them or leave them. I never found a man that made me feel alive before. A man that sort of poured himself into his work, the same way I do. During our many conversations, I found out he felt the same way I do about so many things and he treats me as an equal. I need to be pinched to make sure I'm not dreaming."

Lou said, "You are equal to any man and don't you forget it. I myself want to enjoy everything the world has to offer by enjoying life like a man does and not with my heart on my sleeve. I don't allow any man to make me feel I should or should not react subservient because he is the man. I know you haven't allowed yourself to do anything but revolve yourself around your work. So, I understand why you are surprised to meet a man you are equal to. I envy you for that. As to date, I haven't. Tom and I are having fun and we both like to live and feel alive. I know Tom feels the same way. We take each day and night as it comes and just enjoy the here and now. If it's more than that, only time will tell. I feel Tom is a love'em and leave'em kind of man. I see you looking inside me and I know you are thinking that is exactly what I am, and you are right. I like to be all a woman can be and still have a brain. I prefer to make my own decisions when it comes to my private life. There's something in my private life that allows me to let a man think they know me and but still be able to say goodbye in the morning. I see so many ladies think they are less than a man and forget that we were created equal. Not all men, but so many are using women. Some women feel they need a man to be accepted in society. A crude saying, I have overheard some men say in private to each other on more than one occasion is, 'Oh she is just a friend...you know, one to be used, screwed, and tattooed.' Elaine, we're the lucky ones that know from our parents that we're in charge of our own lives. We can be a follower or we can lead. Never are we to be used, screwed, and tattooed. At least that's what I think Mom was trying to tell us. Our parents are still in love and treat each other as equals and I know for a fact that dad is the kind of man I'm looking for," Lou said.

"I know," Elaine said, "that's why I work and don't play. I never met a man that I considered my equal until Antonio. Funny he feels the same I believe. He and I haven't been together much other than work, yet he feels as I do. We are meant for each other. We are going on a trip and he requested the long way home, so we can get to know each other on a more intimate level. I feel like a little girl in wonderland. I can't wait to start our long way home. I want you and Tom to live, laugh, and love a lot. If something comes of your friendship, take it slow, as you love the life you are living now, but don't let it pass you by either."

Lou said, "That's what I'm sure Tom and I'll do. Start with a friendship and not rush into anything more permanent. Elaine, I put a large package in the Rover. Don't open it until you stay somewhere for the night. I want you to remember to let the woman in you take over; you've been a little girl long enough. All in all, Sis, I have been able to work and enjoy life at the same time. I never did this before, so we both have learned something on this vacation. I'll lock the Sonata in the garage for pick-up. See you in the morning, Sis."

# Chapter 35

The girls got up early and took their showers, did all the things women do in the morning, and went into the kitchen to fix coffee and start the morning off with a smile and a few laughs. Lou fixed both of them cinnamon toast and filled their cups up with coffee. Elaine said, "If Nanny could see us now, she would be so surprised that you know how to make really good coffee. All in all, we've had a busy vacation."

"Tom will be here soon and I have my things packed and have them ready to be loaded in his car for our trip. We'll fly to Hoquiam and then be staying at his home. He said he has some things to check out for Antonio at the restaurant. After that, we'll fly to Malibu. I'm sure we'll stay until you and Antonio arrive. Won't it be fun to have dinner and dancing on a date instead of having to leave on a case?"

"You can say that again! Just a query, Lou: what will you do if Mark finds out you are bringing a friend home to Malibu?" Elaine asked.

Lou said softly in her sexy voice she saves for special occasions to make sure you are listening, "Well, Elaine, what I mentioned before about long friendships, no strings, etc. Mark is one of those. Will I have the same friendship with Tom? Who knows? 'I'm not a kiss and tell person.' I'm quoting a man now. I'm just not ready for any commitment with either Mark, Tom or any other acquaintance of mine. I have a few friendships, but none that were connected to work before; however, Tom, so far is just a friend that happened to fall into the new category. I know I'm having a good time and it's possible that may pass as fast as it started. Who knows? I don't. I'll just enjoy the present and let tomorrow come as it will."

Elaine said, "Well, Sis, I think today just arrived to take you flying...I know it'll be a good flight both in high and low altitude. Stay safe and I'll see you in Hoquiam in a few days." They both wished each other lots of fun and games.

Tom rang the doorbell and when Lou answered, he gave her a hug and kiss and then a hello and smile to Elaine. Elaine thought, *Oh no, there goes that soft voice of Lou's as she said hello to Tom in her own special way.* Tom picked-up the suitcases and took them out to the car.

Lou said, "See you when I see you."

"Okay, Sis, have a great flight. Damn, I wish I had just a little of your sexy moves and that voice, you sure can make a man melt!"

Lou said, "You have a quality about you that demands attention both in your work and in your private life—you just haven't realized it, yet!"

Tom came back and put his arm around Lou and they went to the car. He opened the car door and kissed her lightly. He shut the door, then practically ran around to the driver's side and got in. Elaine thought, *One would think she might not be there if he took his time.* They drove down the long driveway and then Lou rolled her window down, put her head out, and waved. Elaine thought, *Funny she hasn't waved goodbye to me in ages. Is this the start of something new?*

Elaine shut the door and locked it, then went into the kitchen and gave it a once over so whomever cleans the house doesn't think we're bad guests. She checked everywhere in the house to make sure no personal items were left behind. She did her last-minute packing and then loaded the Rover. She notified TIA they could have the cottage back. Everything was locked and ready for the cleaning crew. Lou's car was secured in the garage and ready for pick-up. She called Antonio to let him know she was on her way and would see him shortly.

Elaine drove to the casino and went around back where Antonio was waiting for her. She pulled over and opened the trunk so Antonio could load his things. *Boy, he sure travels light compared to my suitcases she thought as he loaded his one suitcase.* She got out and received a long soft kiss that had the makings of things to come...

Antonio opened her door. As she started to get in, he gave her a light smack on her derriere. She grabbed his hand and said softly, "I kill people for less than that."

As he got into the Rover, Antonio laughed and said, "Honey, I'll remember that and find another way to show my affection for you."

Elaine pulled around to the front of the casino and there was an empty parking place right up front near the entrance. They both got out of the Rover and she heard the doors lock and the security system click in. Antonio said as they held hands and made their way to the cafe, "Just think: this is the first time we have been alone together in the cafe." He held up two fingers to the waitress on duty and she walked them to a booth. "What do you know! Our favorite waiter, Richard, is coming our way with our usual coffee set-up." Antonio thought, *Hmm, the set-up was for two people. How did he know there would be just the two of us this morning?*

Elaine said, "This is the beginning of our long way home. I'm looking forward to the stop in Hoquiam. Lou and Tom are flying there as we speak, but then you know that already."

Antonio had his hand over hers and when Richard returned, he asked him to bring them the breakfast special of the day. He mentioned to Richard they were driving home today and that they would miss his fabulous service.

"Thank you!" Richard said with a wide smile.

Antonio said, "Honey, we can stop wherever you want to on our way back. We'll look for interesting places where we can enjoy ourselves and get to know each other better. We don't need to drive fast unless you find the need to."

Elaine said, "You didn't tell me you were a mind reader!"

"I'm not, sweets; just trying to be romantic," he said as he took a sip of his coffee. "It's been a long time coming for me to show you some romance."

They finished their meal and Richard put the check on the table and removed all but their coffee cups. He returned a short time later with a snack bag for the road. Antonio said, "Thanks for being so thoughtful." "Take care of the young lady and have a safe and fun trip," Richard said.

"I would say someone likes you, dear, or maybe it's the good tips we've always given him. Either way, he earned it," Antonio said. He helped her out of the booth and put his arm around her as they walked to the parking lot.

As they got close to the Rover, she heard the doors unlock and Antonio opened her door, gave her a kiss on the top of her head, and said with a smile, "I'd give you another pat; however, I don't want to be killed. So, look out tonight, kid. I promise nothing but just tender loving care."

He walked around the car and got into the Rover, shut the door, and the safety belt went on automatically. Elaine said, "You have a job to do, dear, as I'm driving. Check on the map and decide where we want to stay this evening and make a reservation. Hopefully."

Antonio said, "I have just the place in mind. I'll layout a plan for this trip if it is okay with you. Also, it would be great if you could teach me some of what this Rover can do on the road."

Elaine replied, "I'll have to ask Bill and if he says okay, we can have some fun and both find out more about what it can really do. What I have found the most fun or I should say important is when it goes into fast mode. We don't have to worry about the highway patrol or any other law enforcement stopping us. We can't use it unless there is a problem ahead and/or have an emergency close by. What I love is the company sends messages to me and if I'm driving in questionable areas, they tell me where to stop, etc. If they call and it's top secret, they have me put on my ear equipment and they will do the talking. That way no one else can know what we're talking about. I keep my answers to yes or no or send them information at the first opportunity. I must always tell them when, where, and why I stop. I'm on their radar (so to speak) at all times."

"That's really interesting and I look forward to getting the okay from Bill to learn more with you," Antonio said.

"How far to Hoquiam?" Elaine asked.

"Funny you should ask. I was going to suggest we not stop overnight on the way back," Antonio replied with a smile. "Not far, dear. We can be there in time for a late lunch and then go to my place. Or do you want to stay at a hotel? Elaine, you choose. I think you'll like my home. It's not a rancho like Tom's. We both have property; however, mine has several features underground, as well as several buildings throughout the property. My home is an updated, modernized home. The outside looks like a country home where one would expect their aged parents to live. I have all the bells and whistles around the property including all the buildings and my entire home. No one can enter the property without credentials including face/eye identity."

"Wow," Elaine said. "What do you have in there that is so valuable, a small Fort Knox?"

"No love, I have all my undercover inventions, what I hear you call goodies, that no one has and that includes your company, TIA. I'd appreciate your complete secrecy to this fact. I'm telling you this on a need-to-know basis, which is between you and me. Since you'll be living with me, you'll have to know the ins-and-outs of my world. By the way, love, I have taken it upon myself to have my contact bring an assortment of rings for you to look at and pick out the one you want. Is that, okay?"

"Are you asking me to be your girl or are you asking me to marry you?" Elaine said, blushing.

"Both, dear; I need to ask your parents first, or is it second...do I ask Nanny Brown first and parents next? Which is it?"

Antonio said. "Let me think about this; you left out my twin sister, Lou," Elaine said.

Antonio said, "Boy, Elaine, next I'll find out I have to ask the Pope."

They both laughed.

It seemed like Lou was whispering in Elaine's ear, *Remember, don't appear too excited.* Elaine said, "Perhaps we should discuss all this tonight at the restaurant. After all Antonio, we are in love and yet we haven't been on a date. Can you believe it? I think my parents and Nanny might wonder if we are nuts or what. Lou on the other hand, knows me so well. She already knows I love you, but perhaps she wants to hear it from you. How about Tom, won't he think you'd better think it over?"

Antonio said, "Honey, I think Tom knew it the first night, when I asked you and Lou to dinner and we danced. I've never done that in my life. In the past all I did was work and I have never made the first move on a woman, if you know what I mean. I've had an evening now and then for fun and games, but the woman always made the first move. Not that I didn't enjoy their interest, but I never really sought their attention. Relationships of the female persuasion were never very important to me, as work took up most of my time and energy. I was too busy fighting the bad guys."

Antonio continued, "You notice I never asked about your love life and that's because you're reserved and yet extremely interesting. Not the type that would say after dinner, 'Your place or mine.' I know that's crude, but men can tell if a woman is genuinely interested in him and not just sex."

Elaine said, "Don't think for a minute women can't tell if you're just a one-time guy. If they want fun and games, they are just taking a page out of a man's book."

"Interesting," Antonio said, "glad you're not an open book; you're just like me. I have a gut feeling this is a lifetime romance. I can't wait till tonight. First the ring, then dinner, and dancing, that is if you'll accept the ring?"

Elaine answered coyly, "I'll let you know at dinner when you give it to me in front of Lou and Tom."

Antonio said, "Honey, if you can put this Rover into overdrive, I vote for getting there quick."

"Sorry Antonio, overdrive is not called for when it comes to personal affairs," Elaine said as she smiled and glanced at him.

"Oh, darn!" he said as he sat back in his seat and closed his eyes. "I'll have to use my imagination until we get there."

# Chapter 36

The ups and downs and many curves in the road were easy to navigate today as the traffic was moving along quite nicely compared to the last time she'd driven it. *Must be a trucker's holiday*, she thought. Elaine looked at Antonio who was just relaxing and said, "Why don't you pour us some coffee and we can pull over or I can drink while I drive. Your call."

He said, "Let's pull over and enjoy the snack Richard packed for us."

"Sounds good to me," as she flashed Bill a message and asked him if it was safe to pull over.

Bill answered, "Come on! Come on! Travel a mile more and there is a clearing which will be checked and ready for you. I'll call you right back if there's a problem."

"Over and out, ole buddy," Elaine said.

"Do you always talk to your handler that way?" Antonio asked.

Elaine said, "Yes, we have for years. I think Bill wanted to be a truck driver in his childhood and hence, he talks like that and I play along. Also, I'll know if someone else answers at which time I'll just ask them to ask Bill to call me when he returns.

Sometimes he will check out things for me that are not necessarily company business."

"You mean, like me?" he asked.

"Well, yes dear, after all a gal has to be careful. Look what happened to the lady on the beach in Hoquiam," Elaine answered.

Elaine signaled and turned off the road into a small area with a picnic tables and restrooms. Antonio removed the bag with all the food and drinks given them by Richard from the back seat. He said, "Excuse me dear," as he stopped and picked a few wildflowers near the table. He gave them to Elaine and they both laughed.

"If I had thought of it, I would have brought a vase," Elaine said.

"One can't have everything when traveling rough. I'll just have to settle for a couple kisses and a toast to our future," Antonio said as he leaned over and kissed her.

Smiling, Elaine poured the coffee and to their amazement, Richard had packed sandwiches, dessert, drinks, plastic cutlery, and napkins.

Antonio said, "Richard thinks of everything, I'm glad I left him a large tip. I still wish I could steal him away from the casino. Alas, my friends at the casino wouldn't look too kindly on that."

The coffee was hot and the food was filling. Antonio said, "And little did I know I was even hungry 'for food, that is.'"

"Keep that thought," Elaine said, "and it might come true."

They finished eating, picked up the trash, and put it in the trash bin. They put the excess food and coffee into the Rover and got in and drove on towards Antonio's home.

Elaine said, "I can hardly wait to see your home."

"Well, as I said, it's an old place. My landscaper keeps the most of the property hidden with flowers and bushes until we get to the road and gate leading up to the main house. He has trees and bushes lining the road, which have cameras and further up some have security restraints that stop anyone that isn't welcome to go back or go forward. Their doors will not allow them to get out of the vehicle. Also, it stops their motor and any mechanical accessories in the vehicle. The house is nothing special to look at until you enter. The home sits high on the property and the spectacular view is all of Hoquiam. You won't be disappointed, love. We should be there shortly."

Antonio continued, "I called ahead and the housekeeper has notified the cook and other staff of our arrival. The landscaper has cleared your Rover for entrance to the property. We'll have them put our things in the suite and we can, when you're ready, walk the property close to the house and later take a ride around the entire property, if that is okay with you?"

"Sounds like a plan," Elaine said.

Antonio said, "I notified the contact for the ring to come to the house instead of the restaurant as previously planned. He can check in at the gate and they'll escort him up. I want to be sure you have the ring you like, as this is forever, dear. When he leaves, we'll go to my workshop and take the necessary steps to add a few features to the ring I have invented that will let me know if you are in trouble, etc. The security feature will never show on any screening, including your company. When we get married, both our rings will have that feature. You'll be able to know my whereabouts, as will I know yours. Elaine, please turn right onto the next intersection. Go about four miles and you will immediately recognize my home. I'm the only home at the end of this road."

# Chapter 37

Elaine went up the road and the gate opened and she continued the drive up a winding road to Antonio's home. The housekeeper and help were waiting out front for them to park and then greet them. "Just park in front of the house by the front door. My man will remove our things and take them to our suite. Ruth my housekeeper will take us to the veranda where I'm sure she will have fresh lemonade and snacks. We can talk there and check out the full view of your new abode," Antonio said.

Music was softly playing in the background and the wind stirred the bushes surrounding the veranda bringing with it a slight fragrance. Combine this with the fresh lemonade and Antonio... romance was in the air.

Ruth came out and asked if they required anything else. Antonio said: "No, thank you Ruth; however, you could bring a tray up to the room with what we couldn't eat right now but will after we freshen up."

Elaine said to Ruth, "I really enjoyed the lemonade; it has a very special taste. What's the secret?"

Ruth blushed and said, "I order lemons from a California orchard where they grow the lemon trees in a well-drained loamy soil high on a hill. They are the best I have found."

Antonio took Elaine's hand and escorted her into the house. They went up the large winding staircase, one where you would expect a grand dame in her best attire to come down, as invited guests watched. The wall at the top of the stairs had an old painting of such a woman. Her hair was pinned up on top of her head with curls cascading down caressing her face. Her earrings and necklace were from years gone by. The neckline of her velvet dress was rather suggestive for that time period. *My kind of girl*, thought Elaine, as she asked, "Who is that lovely lady in the painting?"

"She was the first owner of this home. I don't know who she was, but I just couldn't move it. I'm betting everyone that owned this home felt the same way. Even though I have a modern decor, nothing but that painting could fit there. I should probably say our home is eclectic rather than modern."

Elaine said, "I see what you mean about this painting. It's something I'd invest in even though I don't recognize the painter. I'm sure she had it painted by someone she found interesting as it definitely has a strong feeling that shines through it."

"Bedroom. Perhaps for now, I think we should leave it just the way it is." Antonio showed her where she could put her things and said, "This will be your closet, if it isn't big enough, I'll take care of that."

Elaine laughed, "Oh, it's plenty big enough dear. I haven't acquired a large wardrobe."

Antonio was about to give her a hug when his phone rang.

Elaine chuckled and said, "Take your time. I want to freshen up." She moved towards the ensuite bathroom. She took the package Lou had given her into the bathroom. Elaine took a look at the box and thought, *What in the hell can be so secret?* She opened it and on top of the tissue paper was a note saying: "Just to make you see what a woman should wear when entertaining." There was a silk robe, matching shortie, and high heel slippers in a green/grey blue color. *I don't have her deep green eyes, as a twin I was not so lucky, as my eyes change from shades of gray blue to gray green. This is lovely. I'd never have bought this for myself as the cost for this lingerie would almost be the cost of my entire wardrobe,* she thought and laughed. She undressed and got into the hot shower.

Antonio heard the shower and since the bathroom door was ajar he glanced in and liked what he could see through the fogged over glass doors. He disrobed quickly and entered the shower. . . . Elaine turned around and said, "What a great surprise."

Antonio said softly, "Honey, when I saw the vision of you in the shower, I realized that you are what I desire right now and I couldn't wait for you to finish. Now that I'm here, can I wash your back?"

"Only if I can do the same to you," Elaine said. Her imagination ran rampant, as this was the first time a man had ever washed her back. *I think I could get used to this*, she thought.

Antonio kissed her and pulled her close to him and the rest...is left up to imagination.

Antonio got out of the shower, dried off, took a robe out of the bath closet and went out into the bedroom. Elaine got out and did all the things women do and then slipped into the shortie and long silk robe while stepping into her slippers. She brushed her hair and although her hair was damp, walked out into the bedroom where Antonio was sitting up in the bed. "Can I get you some more lemonade or something else," Antonio asked?

"Well, let's see, can we change that to something else and lemonade later, love?" Elaine said as she slipped into bed and his warm embrace... After slow, tender love making and a short nap, they saw that the time had gone by so fast.

Antonio said, "Let's take a quick shower and then I'll call Tom for dinner reservations."

Elaine was dressed and ready to walk the grounds. Antonio smiled at her and walked over and hugged her tight as he kissed the top of her head lightly and he whispered in her ear, "You are a touch of spring in the thick of winter. You take my breath away!"

Elaine said surprisingly, "My, dear, you're a poet, too, not just a handsome face."

"Would that I was, as I could write a book about my feelings for you," Antonio said softly.

Antonio slipped on his walking shoes and they went downstairs and out the back door and walked towards the first building. "This building is the size of a three-car garage and holds tools that are necessary to use every day in running the household. There is one difference, however: there is a hidden door that leads to a tunnel that takes you from the main house into this building in case one needs a fast escape. You'll notice there is the latest model of motorcycle and a jeep with added features to escape undetected. I can push a button and the tunnel has a fire-resistant steel security door which will close. God help the ones that think they can break through. Pushing the button also automatically drops the same style door at the main house entrance. Ruth and certain employees know about this way to escape danger whether it's a fire, robbery or whatever. There is a fire system, pumped oxygen and emergency lighting both in this building and the tunnel. Staff have orders to just wait until they get an all-clear signal if caught in the tunnel, as the alarm goes on as soon as that door button is pushed. There are four other tunnels from the house, all hidden and secure. I assume this was once a bootlegger's property. However, there are no existing building plans for the outbuildings on this property, for obvious reasons. The woman in the painting at the top of the stairs portrays a certain element of uncertainty and mystery, considering all of the hidden secret passages and hidden doorways on this property. We will probably never know."

"Oh my, a writer could create several books from this ole home if they found out about it," Elaine said.

"Now, Elaine," Antonio whispered, "if you tell anyone about this property and its secrets, as you once told me, 'I kill people for less than that,'" and he laughed as he gave her a pat on her tight looking tush.

"Don't worry, love," Elaine said, "I have better secrets than this ole home; they just aren't from the one I love."

"Well now, kid, that deserves a kiss," as he grabbed her close and their lips lingered on. "I think we'll take the Jeep and drive around instead of walking, as we must meet the jeweler that is bringing the rings for you to select from shortly."

The path/road that went here and there on the property showed different flower beds and bushes with very old stately trees. One area had chairs, tables and a place to dance with tiny lights in all of the surrounding trees and bushes. Elaine thought, *I can imagine in my mind the magical parties they once had here. The lady on the wall and her list of special people. What fun we will have here!*

# Chapter 38

Antonio and Elaine came in just as Ruth was escorting a visitor into the house. Antonio welcomed him and told Ruth to settle him in his study while he and Elaine changed out of their outdoor clothes. On the way upstairs to their bedroom Antonio said, "Elaine my love, pick any ring you like. If he doesn't have what you have envisioned, let him know and we can have it custom made. You know, my love, it's not too late to back out. I can wait until later to announce our engagement if you'd like. I just don't want to call you my 'girlfriend.' I want you as my fiancée and eventually, proudly tell everyone you are my wife."

"I thought we settled that, dear, especially after the afternoon we had," Elaine said glancing at the messy bed. They both laughed and headed back down to the study.

He had the jeweler arrange the jewelry on his rough-edged oak desk. Antonio asked Elaine to select the style she liked so the jeweler could pull out similar ones. "You can see them all if you'd like, it doesn't matter," Antonio said.

"No," Elaine said. "I'll show him what suits me and if you like that style too, Antonio, he can then select those. I'd like one that won't get in the way when I'm on a case, as I go the backroads sometimes myself."

"Dear, you really won't have to do that kind of work anymore or if you want to continue in that line of work, just take the cases you want, like I believe Lou does."

The jeweler took out five trays of lovely diamonds and mentioned, "There are more precious gems I can show you if you don't like diamonds."

Elaine looked and said, "I'd prefer a diamond and believe I'd like one that doesn't have the stone sitting too high on my finger. I wouldn't want to catch it on something or have the stone fall out. I think I'm leaning towards a bezel setting that holds the diamond inside a custom-made thin metal rim that surrounds the outside of the stone, keeping it secure and protected." She looked at Antonio and continued, "You know what work I do, so what do you think? I don't want to have to take it off once you put it on my finger."

Antonio asked the jeweler to show Elaine what he had in bezel settings. He opened his case and pulled out two trays of exquisite diamond rings. Antonio said to Elaine, "Try these on your finger so we can see how high the stones are."
She chose one and slipped it on her finger. Antonio then helped her select the right one. Elaine chose a flawless two carat emerald cut diamond in an eighteen karat yellow gold partial bezel setting. Partial bezel, which left the sides of the bezel open,

allows light to enter the diamond from the sides, making the diamond sparkle brilliantly.

With the choice made, the jeweler gave Antonio the ring which he had placed inside a beautiful sterling silver Tiffany "Elsa Peretti": heart shaped box and said, "May your future be blessed."

"Thank you for your time and help, we are both very happy with our choice of ring!" Elaine said beaming.

Antonio called Ruth on the intercom and had her come and take the jeweler to the front entrance where he would be met by a guard to escort him to the front gate.

Elaine asked Antonio, "Can we wait until we have dinner tonight for you to propose to me, so Lou can give you, her blessing?"

"Wait a minute, dear; I know what they say about twins: if she doesn't approve, please don't tell me 'no,'" Antonio answered.

"Don't worry my love, I make my own decisions when it comes to love. Heavens, she knew I loved you before I even allowed myself to say so."

"Just don't you say 'no,'" Antonio reiterated and then laughed. "Let's go up and get ready for dinner, dancing, fun, and some romance," Antonio said.

He turned off the light in the study and they went to the staircase and started up. Elaine said, "I think that lady on the wall has many secrets! Maybe, one day I'll examine all those hidden areas in our home and find her diary."

Elaine went into the bathroom and brought out the box with more things Lou had put into it for her. She sat on the bed and the next note from Lou said for her to put this on for her first formal date with Antonio. She held it up and it look like something right out of an old movie. A satin three quarter gown in a gray blue color, with lacy personal accessories, shoes to match, and a stole of soft silk in a slightly darker color. *I feel like Cinderella, only I hope I don't lose everything at midnight*, she thought to herself with a chuckle.

Elaine heard Antonio in his dressing room singing. "Not bad," she said softly and went into her dressing room where Ruth had hung up her clothes. Lou had thought of everything. First, she put on the bustier cami lace bodysuit with built in garters, which seamlessly enabled her to attached her French silk stockings. She pulled her gown on and looked in the mirror. The garment melted around her, showing every curve of her supple body. She slipped on her shoes and then draped the stole casually over her shoulders as she had seen Lou do so often and walked into the suite.

Antonio stood there in his black Giorgio Armani tux and said, "You take my breath away."

Elaine said, "Now don't make me cry because no one has ever said that to me before."

Antonio walked over to her and lightly kissed her and said, "That is because no one has ever loved you like I do. Elaine, you are my life now. I knew the very first time you walked into 'Francisco's' and handed me your card with your brilliant smile. You are so beautiful, strong and secure in yourself, honey, and you appeared in my life, an angel from heaven."

Elaine smiled and said, "I'm going to get a diary and write down all of my own personal poet's words. It will be something for us to read when we are old and gray." He took her arm and as the handsome couple walked down the staircase, Elaine pretended she was the lady on the wall. *There's nothing I can't do*, Elaine thought to herself.

In the meantime, Lou was enjoying Tom's hospitality at the rancho. Mama Maria had flowers and food out for her to enjoy while Tom was at the restaurant taking care of business. Lou thought to herself, *I have a good book, food, and drinks in a lovely setting that overlooks all of the town below. How fun it is to just relax and not have a care in the world. It's refreshing to have a nice fellow like Tom for a friend, who makes no demands on me at all. Now this is what I call living.*

She recalled the first time she met Tom and danced the night away. Then she smiled as she thought of Elaine with a man who seemed down to earth and very handsome: *It was obvious from the first dance that they were meant for each other. My Sis has never been in love like this before. I truly thought she would never find love considering how she loves her work and the way she takes so many cases, how could she ever find someone... Well, the good Lord took care of that. I can't wait for Tom to come back; funny I do miss him when he's gone. I enjoy how attentive he is without being possessive. He seems to know what I'm feeling, as I do about him. It's very sexy to be able to be a woman and yet not be expected to perform at a drop of a hat. In fact, that is something to think about.*
Just then there was a touch on her shoulder that was familiar: yes, it was Tom.

"Well Lou, did you enjoy having nothing to do this afternoon?" Tom queried.

"You might say that!" Lou said, looking into his intense eyes with longing.

With that, Tom moved his chair close, leaned over and gave her a soft, long kiss, then said, "That's what I was thinking about all day!"

"Speaking about all day, did it go well and can you stay in Malibu for a few days?" asked Lou.

"I'll know tonight. Antonio has to let me know what he thinks of my plan. Both of us have been working overtime ever since he purchased Francisco's. Between remodeling the restaurant and our homes, we haven't stopped to breath. I can say Antonio has always been like that, but I always found time to relax until we came here. I want to take time off as I know Antonio plans to. If he'll agree to have Mama Maria run the restaurant for a short time, we'll all enjoy Malibu," Tom answered.

"Wonderful!" Lou said. "We'll have fun and I'll show you the sights."

"Hmm," Tom said, "I have an idea, why don't we go to my house and check out the sights there?"

Lou answered, "I would say you read my mind, but my sister is the only one that can do that. I'm glad she isn't here to know what I am thinking."

"That makes two of us!" Tom said smiling as he took her hand and they strolled towards his home.

Tom said, "There was a delivery for you and I took the liberty of having the box put in my bedroom. Now don't tell me: I left you alone for what an hour and already I have another rival?"

"I don't know. I will have to open it," Lou said coyly.

Tom said in a laughing voice, "This time I'll freshen up first and leave you to open your box from your secret admirer. I promise not to ask questions but if you want to tell me what is going on, I'll listen."

Tom went into the ensuite bathroom and Lou proceeded to open the box. It was forwarded to her from Nanny in Malibu. It was from the owner of the boutique in Paris. Nanny wrote in her note, "I took the liberty of sending this package to you. Maybe you will need it."

Lou opened the box and read the note: "This is the latest color of lingerie for this year. I know you like green shades; however, this shade of burgundy with a hint of wine against your skin color, will certainly enhance your green eyes, making them stand out and be even more beautiful than they already are. This small gift is to thank you for making my boutique popular with the jet set in the United States. I have had many orders and they referred to you as having given them my name and address. May this garment bring you luck. Thank you again for your referrals." Lou brushed aside the tissue paper and she was pleasantly surprised by such a beautiful gift.

She told Tom it was okay to come out, as it was a gift of thanks from a shopkeeper in Paris.

Tom said, "That is the first time I've ever heard that excuse."

Lou stood up and held up the lingerie. "Why don't you sit down and I'll model it for you."

"Well sunshine, I think this is going to be a good day after all," Tom said as he poured a drink and sat down.

Lou carried the box into the dressing room and came out modeling the complete set. Tom said, "Let me see all of it."

With that, Lou did the model's walk. She slowly drew open the flowing robe, which when she let the light shine through the sheer material showed her curves within the clinging silk gown that was just tight enough to allow you to imagine the rest.

Tom clapped and said, "Take it off, beautiful. I need to check out what's under the robe."

Lou gracefully walked by him, swinging a side of her robe in his face. Slowly she slipped off the robe and draped it on the chair. Turning slowly, with a light smile and shiny green eyes, she allowed him to see more as she dropped one tiny strap from her shoulder and then slowly let the other strap slide down as she turned with her back to him. The gown slowly slipped down to the floor. She bent over and stepped out of the gown and draped it on the chair along with the robe. All that remained were her burgundy/wine high heels. "Is that enough?" Lou said softly as she turned with her arms crossing her breasts.

Tom walked over and put his arms around her, picked her up and placed her gently on the bed and slowly removed her heels. He undressed rapidly with his back to her and when he turned around, she was waiting for him under the sheets. She beckoned him to join her and spoke in her sexy voice, "I think now you'll have to perform for me."

Tom and Lou cuddled and took a nap after their leisurely love making. When they both woke up, Tom kissed her lightly and held her close. Lou sighed and stayed close. Tom whispered in her ear, breathing at the same time and told Lou, "Now this is a gift I think we both enjoyed."

Lou giggled with a smile on her face and said, "Only if you promise to enjoy the gift again."

Tom had no trouble keeping that promise.

An hour later, Tom looked at the time and said, "Yikes, I can't believe the time went by so fast. We have to get ready for dinner. By the time we shower and dress, we will have just enough time to get to the restaurant to make sure our table is the way I want it. I asked the combo to come in an hour earlier than usual, so we can dance and enjoy ourselves before dinner."

Lou got out of the bed and said to Tom, "We could save time and water if you'd join me in the shower."

"Now that's a very thoughtful plan. I'm always up to finding new ways to help the environment," he said chuckling.

Lou looked in the closet where Mama Maria put her things and selected a silver three-quarter gown with all accessories that matched, even her shoes and purse. Her stole was a combination of silver and green. This time she put on dangling earrings as she had put her long hair in an up-do.

Lou went into the outer room and fixed a drink and glanced at the long accent mirror at the end of the hall to make sure she was put together correctly. "Hmm," Tom said, "who is that lovely lady in silver that brightens up the room? I think I'll have to take an imaginary picture of you so this moment is mine and only mine. Did I say you look like a vision of beauty beyond compare? Am I ever a lucky man or what!"

Lou turned from the mirror and smiled like a cat does when finding catnip. Her eyes sparkled and she slowly walked close to him and softly said, "Are you sure you want to leave just now."

"Hell, no I don't, but between Antonio and Elaine expecting us, we could both be shot if we are late... I have things that have to be done before they arrive. However, Miss Tease, hold that thought for later this evening!"

# Chapter 39

Tom's driver pulled up and was waiting for them to come out the door. He rushed and opened the door for both of them, ran around, got in the driver's seat, and drove slowly down the long driveway. The sun was setting and Tom said, "It is a beautifully natural sight that is never duplicated, much like you when I gaze upon you." The driver slowed down so they could see the sun set slowly into the ocean.

They were taken to the entrance of Francisco's and Mama Maria saw them coming up the stairs and was out the door to greet them. Her smile, especially at Tom, warmed their hearts.

Mama Maria said, "I have everything just right, Tom. I hope it's to your liking? I started the reservations an hour from the time the combo comes in tonight, as you requested. Special flowers on the table and I made sure the arrangement was low enough so all four of you can talk comfortably and not have to look over them. The wine bucket is at the table with ice in it. I placed a rose next to the lady's place settings. Can I do anything else?"

Tom said, "Everything is perfect and I couldn't have done it better myself. I realize now I didn't have to come in so early."

He looked at Lou and said, "Darn, I should have taken you up on what you asked me before we left home."

Lou put her stole and purse by her place setting and she and Tom waited for Antonio and Elaine to arrive. Lou said, "This reminds me of waiting for Elaine when she had her first date to a school dance at the age of fourteen. My shy little sister was ready to faint. She certainly has come a long way since then. She came home and told me: other than dancing, the stupid boy didn't know where to keep his hands and was always trying to kiss her. She then told me she thought she would stick to flying for fun."

Tom and Lou laughed and were still laughing when Antonio and Elaine walked in. Antonio said, "It must have been a good joke."

Tom looked at Lou and said nothing; by then the sisters were hugging and giggling and walking over to the table.

Antonio and Tom stayed by the front desk and were talking to Mama Maria. The business discussion lasted longer than they thought. They looked over at the table where Lou and Elaine were enjoying a glass of wine. At the same time, the combo came in and started to set up their stage. Antonio said to Tom and Mama Maria, "Everything looks great!" Then to Tom he added, "I think we will strike it rich with Mama Maria handling the restaurant while we take time off. Come on, Tom. We better get over to the table before my gal changes her mind."

They both kissed their gals and sat down. The waiter (one of Mama Maria grandson's) delivered the bottle of wine Antonio ordered and opened it. He poured a small amount in Antonio's glass and asked if it met with his approval. Antonio nodded his approval. The waiter asked, "Should I pour or would you prefer to?"

Antonio said, "I believe I'll do it. Thank you."

With that, the waiter put the wine bottle in the ice bucket and left.

Antonio poured wine all the way around and requested they not drink just yet as he had a question, he wanted to ask Elaine. Antonio got on his knee and held up the box with the ring in it. He said to her, "My only love, I knew from the moment I first set eyes on you that I wanted to win your heart! Elaine, will you do me the honor of marrying me?"

Elaine blushed, held out her hand, and said, "How could I say 'no' to my one and only love? I would be honored to call you my husband."

He placed the ring on her finger and they kissed. The combo played softly as Lou and Tom admired her ring. Antonio asked Elaine to join him in the first dance together. They held each other tight and then motioned for Tom and Lou to dance as well. Lou and Tom joined them and danced around the floor like the pros they were. Lou thought, *This is one more thing Tom does so well.*

Mama Maria came over when Antonio and Elaine sat down. Elaine was introduced to her and he told Elaine that Mama Maria was going to be running the restaurant and probably implementing some of her wonderful cooking skills. Mama Maria said, "Congratulations on your engagement, for this special occasion I took it upon myself to give you a bottle of wine we made long before Tom entered our lives. Please accept this as an engagement gift for your good health, happiness, and, always, forgiveness when things go wrong."

Elaine got up and hugged Mama Maria and said, "Thank you Mama Maria. I can see why Lou loves you so much. The food you sent with Lou for our trip to Washington was amazing and we thoroughly enjoyed every bite."

Antonio thanked her for the gift and before he could say anything more, Mama Maria said, "Is there anything more I can do for you?"

Lou and Tom came back to sit while the combo was taking a break. He seated Lou and then hugged Mama Maria. Mama Maria asked, "Are you ready for us to start serving?"

They all said at once, "Looking forward to it."

Antonio said to Elaine, "You are in for a treat; she is the best cook ever. Just think, she will be running Francisco's for us while we are gone."

Mama Maria smiled and went back to the kitchen to give them instructions.

Antonio quickly looked back at the front desk and sure enough one of her granddaughter's was taking care of business. All of Maria's family were dressed alike and always a smile on their faces. *What luck*, Antonio thought, *to be able to leave on a trip and not have to worry about the restaurant.*

Lou was smiling at Elaine and they were chatting between themselves. Tom said to Antonio, "I think we're the luckiest guys in the world. We found ladies that are beautiful, smart, capable, and ours. Well, at least you know Elaine is yours. Lou and I are still playing games, I think."

Elaine thanked Lou for all the lovely things she gave her for this special evening. "Now for you Lou, I had Bill ask Rich to send you a box I hope you will enjoy, with my thanks. It contains things you need for traveling, but in your style. Things that I would call tempting travel gear/clothes."

...ok so lovely tonight you put me to
...ou so happy. Just think, my sister is
and...

...not Francisco's usual food but Mama
...rm cooking—just for tonight. Anti-
...on and on. All fresh food fit for the
...e and removed their dishes and said
...g up soon. Antonio said, "Please tell
we can have one more dance before

Tom got up headed for the dance
...o play a soft love song suited for
people in love. When the dance was over, the waiter returned
with a special dessert that was Mama's secret recipe. Mama
Maria surprised them and came out to serve them personally.
The dessert seemed like a combination between tiramisu, Italian
wedding cake, and zabaglione. Before any of them could ask
Mama Maria about the dessert she said, "No questions, just
enjoy the dessert," and she walked away.

Antonio had the waiter bring a small after dinner liqueur. Tom
got up, holding the liqueur and made a toast to the engaged
couple. Each took a sip and Tom sat down and held Lou's hand
and Antonio kissed Elaine. This is forever love.

The evening guests were coming in and being seated so Antonio suggested that they end the evening in their respective homes and that they would all meet again in Malibu.

The cars were waiting for the four of them. When ready, both drove their separate ways. Elaine looked back and said with a sigh, "This is a night I will never forget!"

"Nor will I," Antonio agreed.

# Chapter 40

Lou and Tom headed back to the rancho and casa. They entered the front room and there package for Lou. "Now just a minute, Lou. Not who knows whom?" Tom said with surprise in

Lou looked at the note on top and it was sealed. all along it was from Elaine, slowly opened it and purse.

Tom said, "Well, missy, just what did that note say?"

"Tom, dear, I am here with you aren't I? What is so strai a box delivered to me or the note? Just another thing f\_ me to look good for you," Lou said.

"It's not important so I think I'll wait until tomorrow to open it," Lou said. She looked at Tom and noticed his face had turned a little reddish. "Oh, come now Tom, nothing to be jealous about. Just another gift from one friend to another," Lou said as she smiled.

Tom said, "You little devil. Let's have a drink."

Lou twisted a strand of her lovely hair. She had an up-do so she removed one hairpin at a time and sipped on her drink.

Tom was watching her and getting excited just seeing her twisting her hair. He thought, *Oh my god, she sure is beautiful. I hope it's up in whatever all I have ever encountered.*

Lou finished her drink, picked up her purse, and took his hand and she guided him towards the bedroom. Lou said with her sultry voice, "This time, Tom, you can take your shower first, you know how women are they like to take time getting ready for bed."

Tom hung up his tux, turned around, and came out to tell her the shower wouldn't be too long— maybe longer if she would like to join him. Before he could say that, he saw Lou sitting on the bed with her gown on the chair. She was taking off her silk stockings one at a time, ever so slowly. She removed one and placed it on the chair and then reached high on her thigh to remove the other stocking, just as slow as the last one. Lou saw Tom from the corner of the mirror so she squirmed a little and reached up to her shoulder, took down the right strap of her bra and then the left, reaching in the back with her hands and undid the bra, placing it by the stockings. She saw Tom coming up from behind as he knelt on the bed behind her...hugged and kissed her neck, back, lips, and softly caressed her beautiful soft body. He gently rolled her over and at the same time pulled the bedding down and placed her under the covers. He gently removed the last of her undergarments as he pressed his body closer to hers. He whispered to her that they could shower together, later. She blew into his ear and her hands touched him softly in a teasing way. They did not speak but enjoyed each other's bodies.

After holding each other close and saying sweet nothings to each other, Lou lightly pushed Tom closer to the edge of the bed and said, "I think you should go take that shower and see if the water can match the warmth we have in bed."

With that, Tom went quickly to the bathroom and got into the shower. Lou followed him into the bathroom and he said, "I know you are there... You better come in and get me warm because I don't think the water is hot enough." Lou opened the door of the shower and grabbed the soap from him and scrubbed him gently and lovingly.

After the shower Tom got out first and took his shorty robe and wrapped it around his torso. Lou took a little more time in the shower and then got out and slipped on her shorty gown. She brushed her hair and twisted the strands so when her hair dried her hair would fall softly on her shoulders. She joined Tom in bed and they kissed good night. *There's nothing like being close after shared time in the bed*, she thought.

The rancho in the early morning was a very busy place. The rooster crowed at sunrise. Someone was feeding the chickens and others were going into the garden to pick fresh herbs and vegetables. The vineyard workers were moving into the grapevine fields, tending to the vines, and checking the grapes.

The intercom rang and Tom answered. It was Mama Maria letting Tom know breakfast would be served in forty-five minutes.

"Lou, dear, it is time to get up for breakfast," Tom said. "

Okay, Tom. I just have to look into the box first," Lou answered.

"Oh that," Tom said.

She came into the living room and he sat beside her on the sofa.

Tom said, "Let's see what your friend sent you."

Lou opened the box and there was a kelly-green traveling skirt, a low-cut silk blouse, boots, and a belt to match; a small travel bag to use instead of a small purse. There was a note in large letters that read: "This is traveling gear for the sky. You and Tom can both enjoy the views."

Tom saw the note and laughed, "You devil. You knew all along what was in the box and who it was from. Just had to make me wonder all night who sent the box."

Lou laughed and said, "It will only take me a few minutes to get into this outfit and then I will be ready for breakfast."

They enjoyed a leisurely breakfast outside on the patio of fresh farm eggs, hash browns, bacon, and fresh fruit.

Lou said, "We have to pack and I can do that fast. I am a pro at packing and unpacking. I first learned how to do that when I was a little girl. Nanny showed us how to pack starting with the first trip to visit our parents. We all work for the same company. My parents, Nanny, and Uncle Harry are semi-retired, but on call. Life is good and interesting. How about you, Tom?"

Tom said, "His life was simple and interesting as well. Antonio and I have been friends most of our lives."

They walked back inside and immediately started to pack. Tom finished fast and had only one suitcase and carry on. He said to Lou that he would call Antonio and give him their itinerary and see if he had any last instructions for him.

"All is clear and nothing important to do but get there safely," Tom said to Lou. She had all her luggage ready and on the front steps.

"I'll call Uncle Harry and have him pick us up at the Santa Monica airport. I said we'd let him know our ETA when we are close to the airport," Lou said.

"Great!" said Tom as his car approached the house. They loaded the car and Mama Maria was there to say good-bye. Lou hugged her and thanked her for making Antonio and Elaine's engagement a huge success and also her great hospitality while she was visiting there. Mama Maria had tears in her eyes as Tom hugged her and told her to look after things. They got into the car as they were driven down the long road to the airport.

Lou said, "Tom I have to tell you, this is the most fun I've had on a vacation in some time. Thank you so much!"

# Chapter 41

Antonio and Elaine packed the Rover and they were on the road again. He leaned over and gave her a kiss and said, "That is one for the road."

They laughed and after the Rover was warmed up and ready to drive, she said, "Thank you love for everything. My ring shines so lovely when the sun hits it through the window."

Antonio replied, "I'm so glad you found the one you liked, just think if you hadn't, we would have had to stay another day so we could get the one you wanted. Remember, I know where you are at all times because I took the ring to my workroom and altered it. Even your company will not be able to detect anything. There are only three people that have a ring with those qualities: you, me, and Tom. When we get married, I will fix our rings to allow both of us to know where we are at all times. I would like our private lives to remain private. The world is a large place and with today's technology, people can know everything about everyone. Today I think we find ourselves being listened to by gadgets that allows them to keep track of what you buy, what you like and what you said, even when you do not know it.

"There is artificial intelligence (AI) out there that has the wherewithal to know all about you—even help our school children with their supposed homework and essays, etc. They give information they want the children to know and not necessarily the truth. AI slants things the way they want one to perceive them to reflect their way of thinking. If our people keep being led instead of thinking for themselves, some less fortunate people will become mindless fools and believe the hype that is thrown their way, later to find out they are stuck by not using their own brains and common sense. When we have children, we will have someone like Nanny to educate, not manipulate. That is if it isn't too late. Hence, we must find out what these conferences are all about."

Elaine spoke up, "I agreed with your feelings and be assured that what happens in our home stays private. For our eyes and ears only."

Just then there was a flash on the dashboard. It was from Bill. Elaine put it on speaker. Bill said, "Come on, come on!"

Antonio and Elaine chuckled.

Bill continued, "First, I just want to congratulate the both of you on your engagement. Secondly, I have an update on the parents of Mary Ann's friend Carol. We checked their credentials and employment history as you suggested Elaine. Elaine, you were right-on again: her father is a very important person when it comes to Taiwan. He is expected to be the CEO of the new plant that the Taiwanese government is building in Arizona. Maybe it wasn't Mary Ann from the university they wanted but her roommate Carol, who is the daughter of that CEO. No wonder you wanted me to have the RV followed. So far, the parents in the RV are following their itinerary and not deviating from their route. We have now called the different law enforcement agencies in route to confirm their location when seen in their specific areas. However, no one is to in any way let them know they are being watched. Our many traveling agents are both in front and back of them. Others are stationed at the RV parks they mentioned they were going to stay at when they stop for the night. According to our calculations, we know approximately where they will need to stop for gas.

"We have prearranged for agents to be on alert for anyone that might want to kidnap any one of them. We are keeping our eyes on the girls because they always get out of the RV and walk around whenever the opportunity presents itself. It seems the parents stick close to the RV unless they go into the stores to purchase essentials.

"We contacted Mary Ann's parents in Germany and discussed their inviting Carol to join Mary Ann in Germany to finish the year at the university in Germany. Carol will get special credits if she does. They have agents in place to look after the students.

"That leaves the CEO and his wife of the new plant in Arizona easier to protect without their daughter present. TIA has a guest safe house (with all the goodies and bugs) that we'll have the Arizona officials handling the project for the Taiwanese government give them to use with the excuse that it comes with the project. They will explain that they will be closer to the site as well as they won't have to pay the high rental prices it costs to stay in the best area in Arizona. Do you have any questions or suggestions?"

Elaine looked at Antonio and he shook his head.

Elaine said, "You're doing a great job Bill and we're glad they are being watched. Bill, we plan to go to Malibu and make arrangements to go to England to visit my parents. Antonio and I want to plan our wedding as soon as possible. It'll be very private affair with just immediate family on one of our estates. Please notify the powers that be. I will want time away from work. Just how long remains to be seen. Right now, we are Malibu bound and if we hit traffic can I contact you and fast track the Rover to bypass all traffic?"

Bill replied, "Just let me know and it'll be done."

Elaine added, "Oh, Bill. How far is that restaurant from here, the one Lou and I had dinner at that you recommended? Do you know if they are open for brunch?"

Bill said, "I'll check it out and let you know. Also, I'll make arrangements to have the both of you fly to England on a non-stop flight when you let me know when you plan to leave for England. Stay safe and call if you need me. Over and out."

Elaine said, "Ten-four, good buddy!" And the dash went dark.

Antonio smiled and said that this was a good set-up when one was on the road. "Thanks for allowing me to see what happens when you hit traffic or have to get somewhere for the company."

Elaine asked Antonio, "Can you wait for a late breakfast or lunch. This restaurant Lou and I ate at is the best place to eat in this area and it's anything but a fifties diner. Great service and the food is delicious. It's private and we don't have to worry about security."

"Sounds good," Antonio agreed.

They headed towards California and the dashboard flashed a message: "*About seventy miles to the fifties dinner and they are open. I made reservations and they will hold the table for your arrival. Check has been paid for in advance including the tip. The company said to stay safe and don't talk to strangers, the usual.*"

Elaine said, "Here we go now, love. This road starts with so many ups and downs and large curves. This is where Lou tried to close her eyes so she wouldn't get car sick. I'm so used to driving everywhere or as you call it 'taking the back roads.'"

Antonio suggested again that she think over taking back road cases. He said, "You have earned the right to be selective. I know the challenge is what gives you a high. It certainly did me. Let's face it: you are great at your job. But now that we are going to marry, we have to prioritize what we do."

They both were getting hungry when a message came on the dash: *"One mile ahead turn right to the diner."*

"OMG, am I ready to eat!" Elaine said to Antonio.

She checked her mirrors and pulled safely over into the right lane, pulled off, and parked in front. Antonio got out and went around and opened the door for Elaine. "Thank you dear," Elaine said, as the door shut and the locks went on.

They went into the diner and Antonio realized what Elaine meant when she said it wasn't a normal fifties diner. They were seated and the waitress took their orders and a bus boy placed the napkins on their lap. "There is food and coffee to go when you are finished. It has also been taken care of," the bus boy said.

"Thank you," Antonio said. They ate and shared conversation. When they got up to leave, Antonio left another tip for the waitress and gave one to the bus boy as he passed by. "I know that when the company pays the check in advance the tip is not in accordance with the service received," he said. They both took a pit stop before leaving for the car. When Elaine came out Antonio was waiting at the door. They went to the Rover and it unlocked and they both got in.

Elaine looked at Antonio and said, "I hope the trucks are not backed up as much as they were the last time." She pulled out onto the highway and continued on their way. They were about an hour out and a message came on the dash: *"Fast drive available now. When you want you to go back into regular mode indicate it on the dash. You know the drill."* She looked at Antonio and said, "This is going to be fun. Well, not fun except watching the trucks all move over and the road is ours. Much like fire trucks, etc."

After about a mile they encountered the traffic having pulled over and no one in the left lanes. Antonio said, "This is great. There are no on- or off-ramps so no one is inconvenienced except the trucks and then, if the trucks follow the speed limit, even they can't complain."

Elaine said, "It's like flying in low altitude," and they both laughed.

The turns in the road let up and they really went fast, traveling a long way in half the time. The dash flashed and a message came up: *"Time to turn off the fast mode as there are more towns starting to pop up. Hope you enjoyed your system of transportation. Stay safe and in thirty miles stop and fill your tank. Over and out Bill."*

They stopped for gas and ate some of the food from the diner. They hoped they would be able to drive non-stop for most of the way back to Malibu if they decided they wanted to go straight home.

The dash message came up and Bill indicated if Elaine wanted to rest from driving Antonio has been cleared to drive the Rover. He has to place his hands on the wheel for thirty seconds so it could read his palm and fingerprints. After doing this once, he'll be able to drive the Rover whenever it's necessary. Antonio said, like a little boy, "Oh can I? Please, can I, can I?"

Elaine laughed and said, "If you're a good boy and do whatever I ask of you tonight, then sure you can drive."

Antonio looked at her as she pulled over at the side of the road and he said, "Honey, just say the word and I'll follow you anywhere and do whatever you desire."

# Chapter 42

She stopped the vehicle, making sure she was far enough on the shoulder of the highway so she could get out safely. Antonio was out and around the Rover and opened the door for her. She got out and went around the back of the car and as she got in the passenger side, Antonio was already waiting with his hands on the steering wheel.

Antonio looked at her and said out loud, "Look out, world, here we come." He checked the oncoming traffic and made sure it was safe to pull out.

"This is a great car. I could drive this mother a long way. Your body fits the seat well and it also automatically adjusts for my legs with the correct distance for me to relax and not get cramps. Now this is a super-duper driving machine, girl."

Elaine laughed and said, "It sure is. I think I'll close my eyes for a while and you can let me know when you'd like me to take over."

After a time, she woke up and they were to Ventura already. "OMG, I'm sorry I fell asleep for so long."

Antonio said, "That's okay, dear. I'm really enjoying driving this car. I want to stop for gas and make a pit stop."

She agreed and said she would drive from there as she knew the way to her home.

Antonio pulled into the gas station, filled the tank, went inside the station, and came out with two cups of coffee.

Elaine got into the driver's side and they proceeded towards home. "I called Nanny and told her where we are and she said they will wait for our arrival to eat. Lou, Tom, and Harry are already there. She said they would occupy their time waiting with a walk, conversation, and some laughs. I said I would call her when we are closer."

Antonio laughed and said, "Your Nanny sounds so lovely."

Elaine replied, "Yes, we were so lucky to have her as a Nanny. Actually, she is our second mom. I always call before arriving so she can have the cook and his help take care of everything. I know she will be sorry to see us leave for England so soon and I think Lou will be going back to work after Tom leaves. Nanny and Harry will be by themselves, then. She did mention that they might fly to England for some kind of get together with other retired professors."

Elaine added, "I can tell you now, dear, that I'm sure Harry and Nanny were in Ocean Shores at the same time we were. I think Nanny Brown was undercover for the company and worked as a clerk and cashier. When Harry and Nanny worked for TIA, they were noted for their disguise ability. I know if she was in Ocean Shores, Harry was also. She slipped up when she waited on me and would have gotten away with it if it wasn't for her saying as I was ready to leave checkout that I should take a look at the sunglasses they have for sensitive eyes. No one but Nanny knew I have sensitive eyes. I said nothing and purchased two pairs. One for me and one to give Nanny when we get home. A personal joke between us."

Antonio laughed and asked, "What made you think Harry was there?"

Elaine answered, "First of all, Nanny has never been undercover without him. Second, after the sunglasses episode, I watched the waiter Richard. He couldn't help but look after Lou and me. We are as close to being their children as anyone. I didn't tell Lou, but I believe she suspected this as well."

Elaine spoke to the dash and said, "Contact Nanny and let her know we are fifteen minutes out." They drove up to the front steps of the Malibu estate where all four of them were waiting. They ran down to greet us with hugs all the way around. Nanny was so happy, she had tears in her eyes. It was love all the way around.

Nanny said, "We should all go to the patio overlooking the ocean. They will be bringing out the food shortly."

Elaine said, "We'll be there after we take our things up to my room."

Lou said, "Go ahead, we will pour the drinks. Make it fast."

Elaine took Antonio's hand and he follow her up the stairs carrying the suitcases that Elaine hadn't grabbed. She had Antonio open the door to her suite. The first thing he noticed was her exercise equipment. He laughed and said, "No wonder you liked my suite. You were not kidding when you said it was like mine. Honey, we sure are going to have a great life!" They set down the suitcases and went back downstairs to the patio.

Lou handed each of them a glass of the special wine Mama Maria had given Antonio and Elaine for an engagement present. Lou said, "Elaine gave it to me before we left to be sure all of us could enjoy it." Uncle Harry and Nanny held their glasses up and said a toast to the soon to be newlyweds. Elaine held back her tears and Antonio put his arm around her and kissed her lightly on the head. Tom and Lou held up their glasses and toasted to their future and all the wonderful things marriage can bring.

Antonio said, "Thank you from the bottom of our hearts. Now may I suggest we start the buffet before Elaine faints?" Everyone chuckled and commenced eating.

After eating, they all went out and watched the sunset where they saw a green flash as the sun went into the ocean. *How special,* everyone thought. A great climax to a to a wonderful evening. They went into the living room and sat down to enjoy an after-dinner drink. They sipped and talked getting to know each other better when the phone rang. Nanny answered the call and nodded towards the twins motioning that the call was for them.

The girls got up and went to the office and put the phone on speaker. Bill said, "Elaine, this is short notice but is it possible that you and Antonio could be at the Santa Monica airport tomorrow at 3:00 p.m.? TIA has their jet leaving for a non-stop flight to England."

Before asking Antonio, Elaine said, "We'll be there."

"Lou, we have a case we'll need you to take if you want—in three or four days. You can fly first class as usual."

Lou said, "That would be good. I'll call you when I plan to leave and TIA can make the arrangements for me."

"Elaine, we have notified your parents and they will send their limo for you and Antonio."

"Thank you," they both said and the phone went dead.

Lou said, "Well, Sis, it was fun while it lasted," and they headed back to the living room.

Lou went into the room and sat next to Tom. Antonio walked over to Elaine asked, "Is everything alright, Elaine?"
Elaine explained what the company wanted and said, "I hope you're not upset with me, Antonio, but I answered like I always do and said 'yes.' We have to leave tomorrow to go to England and we must be at the airport at 3:00 p.m."

"Honey, of course it is okay. I want to meet your parents as soon as possible and arrange our wedding." They gave each other a light kiss.

Lou said to Tom, "I have bad news as well. Instead of staying here a week or so I find I have to leave in three to four days."

Tom took her hand and looked her in the eye and said, "I guess we have to make the most of the next couple of days."

Antonio said, "You have something for Nanny, I think. You can walk up to your room with me and come back down to talk to Nanny and Harry."

Antonio said to Tom, "While the ladies talk to Nanny and Harry we can discuss a few things for you to handle for me while I am gone."

Lou stood up and told Tom that she needed to get something in her room and they can talk while Elaine comes back down.

"Okay, sounds good to us," they all said.

There stood Nanny and Harry and they said they would have a sweet drink with Lou and Elaine.

Lou got into her suitcase and took out a little something for Uncle Harry while Elaine got out what she had purchased at Ace Hardware for Nanny. The sisters met at the top of the stairs with a small package in their hand. They asked Nanny and Uncle Harry to sit down for a minute. "We want to thank you for all you do for us. You go first Sis," Lou said.

"Okay, here goes nothing," said Elaine. She had Nanny hold out her hand and was given a small package. Nanny opened it and it was a pair of sunglasses. "Nanny these are for 'your' sensitive eyes," she said as she winked.

Nanny started laughing and they looked at Uncle Harry and Lou.

Lou said "Hold out your arm," and he did; she opened the tissue paper wrapped gift. She placed it on his arm and Lou said, "Thank you for being the best waiter ever," and she placed a white towel over his arm.

Nanny and Uncle Harry said they have changed their looks and even the best agents could not tell it was them, and they were trying. "You two discovered us fast. No, not by your looks but by the love for us coming through."

"Little things, you both said. For that we would like to thank you and that we love you."

Harry gave them a small drink to close the night.

"Until tomorrow," Nanny and Uncle Harry said. "To all of us," they said, and drank and put their glasses down and walked up the stairs for a good night's sleep.

Antonio was waiting for Elaine.

Tom was waiting for Lou.

Nanny and Harry both went into their suite.

Ahh, all is right with their lives now. . .

But what about a year from now?

# Acknowledgements

The author wishes to thank my dear friends who critiqued this book.

Special thanks to the cover model, Harmony.

Many thanks to and undying gratitude to Rodney Bertram, graphic designer, for endless computer assistance.

To my friends from Arizona, California, Florida, and New York.

Printed in the USA
CPSIA information can be obtained
at www.ICGtesting.com
CBHW021754100724
11116CB00001B/2